"Lost River" *is an extraordinary work of art. It is a story of death and rebirth, borrowing from myth and fairy tale, but also conjuring up literary texts from* Frankenstein *and* Dracula, *from Southern Gothic to Magical Realism. Yet it remains entirely itself, not quite like anything else I've read. The prose is rich and delicate, the characters memorable, the story immersive. It has the feel of an instant classic.*
Anthony McGowan, Carnegie Medal Winner for *Lark* and Leapfrog Global Fiction Prize YA Judge 2021.

LOST
RIVER
1918

LOST
RIVER
1918

FAITH SHEARIN

TSB & LEAPFROG PRESS
LONDON AND NEW YORK

Lost River, 1918
9 8 7 6 5 4 3 2 1

First published in the United States by Leapfrog Press, 2022

Leapfrog Press Inc.
P.O. Box 1293, Dunkirk, NY 14048
www.leapfrogpress.com

First published in the United Kingdom by TSB, 2022

TSB is an imprint of:
Can of Worms Enterprises Ltd
7 Peacock Yard, London SE17 3LH
www.canofworms.net

© 2022 Faith Shearin
Photo credit: © Gordon Kreplin

Cover and text design: James Shannon
Set in Baskereville and Solander

ISBN: 978-1-948585-51-4 (US paperback)

ISBN: 978-1-911673-22-4 (UK paperback)

About the Author - Faith Shearin

Lost River, 1918 is Faith Shearin's first published novel, and the winner of the inaugural Leapfrog Global Fiction Prize for Young Adult fiction. Faith has published numerous books of poetry including: *The Owl Question* (recipient of the May Swenson Award), *Moving the Piano* (SFA University Press), *Telling the Bees* (SFA University Press), *Orpheus, Turning* (Dogfish Head Poetry Prize), *Darwin's Daughter* (SFA University Press), and *Lost Language* (Press 53). Her short stories have appeared in *The Missouri Review, Meridian, Literal Latte, Atticus Review, Frigg* and *Bellevue Literary Review* among others.

Faith has received awards from Yaddo, The National Endowment for the Arts, The Barbara Deming Memorial Fund and The Fine Arts Work Center in Provincetown. Recent work has been read aloud on The Writer's Almanac and included in American Life in Poetry.

Of the writing process for *Lost River, 1918*, Faith Shearin writes:
"I wrote the first chapter of *Lost River, 1918* during a blizzard in West Virginia, where I lived for six years in relative isolation, on top of North Mountain, near Harpers Ferry, with my daughter and husband. That chapter sat on the desktop of my computer for two years and I returned to it in 2019, after my husband died of a heart attack at the age of 48. I wrote most of Lost River during a time of grief, creating a landscape where the dead and the living could speak to one another. As I was writing the final chapters in my daughter's abandoned bedroom (she had left for college) I felt the presence of all my family ghosts, including my late husband, leaning close. The story helped me survive. I finished the manuscript one month before Covid broke out and was amazed afterwards at how the world around me erupted in contagion just as it had for the Van Beests in 1918."

Production and Publishing Credits

A considerable number of people are involved in realising an author's work as a finished book on the shelf of your local library, bookshop or online retailer. TSB and Leapfrog Press would like to acknowledge the critical input of:

Leapfrog Global Fiction Prize readers and judges. Our first thanks go to all those who submitted their work to the Leapfrog Global Fiction Prize in 2021 and to our indomitable readers for whittling down the entries to our longlist. Carnegie Medal winning author, Anthony McGowan, judged the finalists and this work, *Lost River, 1918* was chosen as the inaugural winner of the Young Adult category prize.

Cover design. TSB/Can of Worms has benefitted from a longstanding relationship with James Shannon on book production and website development for many of its own titles as well as some of Can of Worms's consultancy clients. James and further examples of his work can be found at: www.jshannon.com

Illustration. The chapter head illustrations are of Ghost Pipes or *Monotropa Uniflora* and created by Dana Falconberry and feature prominently in *Lost River, 1918*. https://danafalconberry.com/collection/ghost-flower-triptych

Typesetting. Typesetting has been provided by Prepress Plus, New Delhi, India (http://www.prepressplus.in) based upon a template created by James Shannon. The text has been set in Baskerville, a transitional serif typeface designed in the 1750s by John Baskerville (1706–1775) in Birmingham, England. The cover and headline font is Solander.

Editorial. Editorial has been overseen by Rebecca Cuthbert, managing editor of Leapfrog Press and Shannon Clinton-Copeland. Tobias Steed is publisher of Leapfrog Press and TSB | Can of Worms. Tobias's career in publishing has spanned forty plus years having started as an editorial assistant for Johns Hopkins University Press in Baltimore, co-founder with Chris Burt and Magnus Bartlett of illustrated travel guides publishing company, Compass American Guides, Oakland, California, Associate Publisher and Director of New Media at Fodor's/Random House, New York.

Sales and Marketing. Sales and Marketing for all Leapfrog Press titles in the US and Canada is overseen by Consortium Book Sales and Distribution (CBSD) St. Paul, Minnesota 55114 www.cbsd.com. Sales and Marketing for all TSB | Can of Worms titles is overseen by Garry Manning of The Manning Partnership. Garry also oversees the TSB | Can of Worms relationship with our distributor, GBS/Penguin Random House. www.manning-partnership.co.uk

Publicity. All publicity enquiries should be directed to Tobias Steed, publisher in the UK info@canofworms.net and Mary Bisbee-Beek in the United States mbisbee.beek@gmail.com.

Further information can be found at www.canofworms.net and www.leapfrogpress.com

Acknowledgements

Thanks to Anthony McGowan and everyone at Leapfrog/ Can of Worms Press for believing in this book. Thanks to Rebecca Cuthbert for her gentle editing and attention to detail. Thanks to Mary Bisbee-Beek for her publicity insights. Thanks to Tobias Steed for helping this story find its way into the world.

I am grateful to Lucy Rosenthal and Gloria Whelan for encouraging me to write fiction.

I want to thank my brilliant daughter and emissary, Mavis Murdock, and remember her father, my late husband, Tom; I want to thank Tucker Windover, who taught me to see life in the river, and remember his brother, Fred Barnicoat; I want to thank my friend Bonnie Croskey and remember her sister, Corinne; I want to thank my friend Justin Robertson and remember his sister, Heather; I want to thank my teacher, Jack Driscoll, and remember his wife, Lois; I want to thank Daniel Bond for being my husband's friend, then mine, and remember his father, Alan; I want to thank Melanie Sumner and remember her husband, David; I want to thank Joan Windover for welcoming me and remember her husband, Fred Alvah; I want to thank Adrienne Su and remember her father, Kendall; I want to thank Carol Murdock and remember her husband, Jerry; I want to remember my ghost dog, Turtle, and North Mountain, where we could see everything and nothing; I want to remember my grandfather, Henry, who loved me the way the earth loves a potato.

Thank you to Margaret Atwood for her MasterClass, and to Uncle David McLelland for his witty missives and his kindness. Thank you to Anna Georgiopoulos and Mike Manzella for years of true friendship. Thank you to Garrison Keillor and Ted Kooser for helping my writing find its audience. Thank you to my poetry friends: Kareem Tayyar, B.A. Van Sise, and Taylor Mali. Thank you to Dava Sobel for her humor and warmth.

Thank you to John Skoyles and Mark Brazaitis for years of literary friendship.

Thank you to my family, whose inability to conform has been a blessing: Dana Shearin and Wesley Owen, Wilson and Ben Shearin, and my parents Anne and Norman Shearin, who believe in dreams.

Thank you to my grandmother, Ruth, for telling me the story of an aunt on her father's side who died of the Spanish Flu, and whose ring slipped through floorboards, into lore.

**LEAPFROG
GLOBAL
FICTION
PRIZE**

Faith Shearin's *Lost River, 1918* and *My Sister Lives in the Sea* were judged to be joint winners of the inaugural 2021 Leapfrog Global Fiction Prize for Young Adult | Middle Grade fiction. Judge of the 2021 contest and Carnegie Medal Winner, Anthony McGowan, said of *Lost River*:

Lost River is an extraordinary work of art. It is a story of death and rebirth, borrowing from myth and fairy tale, but also conjuring up literary texts from Frankenstein and Dracula, from Southern Gothic to Magical Realism. Yet it remains entirely itself, not quite like anything else I've read. The prose is rich and delicate, the characters memorable, the story immersive. It has the feel of an instant classic.

Past Winners of the Leapfrog Global Fiction Prize
(*denotes Young Adult | Middle Grade titles)

2021: *But First You Need a Plan* by K.L. Anderson
2021: *My Sister Lives in the Sea* by Faith Shearin*
2021: *Lost River, 1918* by Faith Shearin*
2020: *Wife With Knife* by Molly Giles
2019: *Amphibians* by Lara Tupper
2018: *Vanishing: Five Stories* by Cai Emmons
2018: *Why No Goodbye?* by Pamela L. Laskin*
2017: *Trip Wires: Stories* by Sandra Hunter
2016: *The Quality of Mercy* by Katayoun Medhat
2015: *Report from a Place of Burning* by George Looney
2015: *The Solace of Monsters* by Laurie Blauner
2014: *The Lonesome Trials of Johnny Riles* by Gregory Hill
2013: *Going Anywhere* by David Armstrong
2012: *Being Dead in South Carolina* by Jacob White
2012: *Lone Wolves* by John Smelcer*
2011: *Dancing at the Gold Monkey* by Allen Learst
2010: *How to Stop Loving Someone* by Joan Connor
2010: *Riding on Duke's Train* by Mick Carlon*
2009: *Billie Girl* by Vickie Weaver

These titles can be bought in the United States and Canada online at:
https://bookshop.org/shop/leapfrog

These titles can be bought in the United Kingdon online at:
https://uk.bookshop.org/shop/TSB_CanOfWorms

Please support your local bookshops whenever possible.

For my grandmother, Ruth Spruill, and my parents, Anne and Norman Shearin

And in memory of the dead: Thomas Murdock, Henry Grayson Spruill, Norman and Annie Belle Hall Shearin, Irene Cherry and Henry Wayland Spruill who first told me stories about 1918, Uncle Bill Spivey, Lucius and Doreen Shearin, Martha Hinnant and William Jasper Hall, Helen and Joseph Spivey and the sons they lost in the Second World War: Joseph, James, and Lowell

Table of Contents

Chapter One

The living are concerned with houses, and clocks, and fine dining, while the dead, unmoored, drink moonlight and shadows. Our story begins in the place where night becomes morning, when our mother, Ariel, was delivering a baby. She had ridden away, into the twilight, with a nervous young father, and would return to us with a bundle of silence. I remember the way the expectant father stood on our porch, with his hands in his pockets, his eyes as dark as winter. This was 1918, in West Virginia, on North Mountain, where the crooked Victorian we inherited from our father's Aunt Nora sat at the edge of a rippling wilderness. In this place, death moved in rivers and slept in caves; it rustled in meadows and orchards, and climbed into the branches, beyond the windows of the room where my sister, Frannie, and I slept under heavy quilts.

We were used to death and life moving around us. Our father, Fergus, was a mortician. We had seen the stiff bodies of our neighbors, in pine coffins, laid out for viewing in our parlor: the bodies of men who worked in mines, or their tired wives; sometimes dead children appeared on our porch—victims of pneumonia, consumption, diphtheria—and Frannie and I pulled back our bedroom curtains to examine them, wrapped in quilts or sheets. Our mother, Ariel, was a midwife; she visited the cabins in Darkesville where life emerged. Our father tended death, while our mother welcomed life. They had inherited these professions from their own parents on an island off the coast of North Carolina where both branches of our family—the Van Beests and the Flynns— had resided for more than a century. Frannie and I noticed that the living were frightened of the dead, and the dead watched the living from their unlit acres, offstage. Our father said the dead wanted what gardens want and what seasons want. Frannie and I did not understand what he meant by this.

We had not lived long in West Virginia. The forest that crept up our mountain and extended, in both directions, around us was deep with trees we'd never seen. These were not the Southern Pines we had known in North Carolina, or the Weeping Willows that dreamed beneath long, green waterfalls of hair; they were not the Cypress trees, hunched over their own exposed roots, heavy with moss. They were not Cedar of Lebanons: those ancient cathedrals with ladders to the sky. These trees were thick, and twisted, with leaves so big that, when they fell, we mistook them for animals; their white bark glowed in the moonlight. We had no proper name for them though the gypsy travellers called them *Clotho* after the Greek Fate who weaves the web of our lives when we are born. There were stories about these trees: how they connected the world of the living to the realm of the dead; ghosts were known to sleep in their canopies, calling to one another like birds. Beyond the trees, on a nearby mountaintop, was a bog in which bodies had been discovered, perfectly preserved: their hair neatly combed, the fabric of their shirts intact, their hands still holding a locket or knife. There was a cave to the west of Lost River that was said to serve as a door between worlds, a place where ghosts gathered like fireflies.

To live on North Mountain was to live where the dead appeared in places other than abandoned houses or cemeteries or dreams.

Our mother had been away all night and our father, Fergus, was in the barn, fixing hinges on coffins. Frannie and I woke up in our bed, beneath thick quilts, where we slept with our pet squirrel, Speck; he had built a den for himself, between our pillows, using socks. As a baby, Speck fell from his nest, and our mother allowed us to rescue him. Frannie and I fed him scrambled eggs from a spoon, and nuts and berries and, after a while, he emerged from his blankets to dart around our room. He climbed up the legs of our desk and raced along our headboard; in most weather we opened our windows, so Speck could come and go, because he was both wild and domesticated: a member of our family, and a member of the kingdom of rodents. Speck had four teeth at the front of his mouth, and soft feet; his fur was brown with bits of white; his tail was lively.

Frannie and I ate bread with jam from the cupboard in the kitchen, and put on our sweaters, because summer had ended, and the mornings were cooler now. We went into the forest to play. Speck slipped into the forest too, though we did not often see him there, because he could run faster than we could, and climb higher, his tail like a flame. In those days, Frannie and I liked to act out stories from our Grimm book of fairy tales; these were the stories our father, Fergus, read to us at night, when shadows were cast by our fireplace, where flames rippled. Our father sat by the window, in a deep chair, turning the pages of a book, and the window glass was black so he was reflected there: his chocolate eyes and beard, his lantern. He said we should write our own book of fairy tales and give it our last name, Van Beest, and I sat sometimes in my bedroom, with my Esterbrook fountain pen and pocket notebook that had been a gift from my Grandpa Willem when I left North Carolina, drawing pictures of forests, and imagining stories that involved curses and spinning wheels. I did whatever our father suggested because his love was like sunlight; Ariel loved us with corrections; she loved us with the spit she used to wipe away dirt or food stains, but Fergus loved us the way the earth loves a potato.

On this day Frannie and I decided to be Hansel and Gretel, only we both wanted to be Gretel because she was the girl.

"It's my turn," Frannie said and I did not argue. Still, I hated being Hansel; he was such a fool.

We found a place in the forest where the white trees left a circular space for us beneath their over-sized falling leaves, and began to perform the story of children abandoned in the woods, and rooftops made of candy, and birds eating the bread we dropped from our pockets, until the road home became more and more mysterious. In one scene, I was Hansel, and I was also the Witch, feeling my own finger to see if it had fattened; in the middle of our performance we heard hooves on packed mud and knew our mother was returning. Ariel was often tired but happy after a birth. She made lunch, and told us about the new mother, and the details of the baby and its arrival. Then she went to bed for a long time, the curtains drawn, and Frannie and I knew to be quiet. But, on this day, Frannie and I saw our mother standing with our father on the front porch, and she carried a bundle the size of a baby, which she passed to our father, who disappeared into the barn, which had a room at the back where he tended the dead.

Our father, Fergus, learned his trade from his own father, who had also been a mortician, further south, on an island near the sea, where bodies were warmer, and wetter, and harder to preserve. Fergus knew how to make coffins and headstones; he knew how to take photographs of the deceased, in which they sat upright or appeared to be sleeping. Our father kept embalming fluids in the loft of our barn: arsenic, zinc, creosote, turpentine. He kept a stack of coffins along the north wall, though none was small enough for a baby.

Frannie and I had seen at least a dozen dead babies in our father's funerals, which often took place in our own front parlor. Our Great Aunt Nora, who left our house to our father, had been a lonely, remote woman who wore high collars and brooches and her parlor had unforgiving furniture, grandfather clocks, and red carpeting. It contained an imposing grand piano. Funerals for babies were white: white flowers and candles, a white dress for the infant, ostrich plumes, white gloves, the coffin itself painted white; we knew the rules of death:

how curtains were closed, and clocks were stopped, how mirrors were obscured by veils, and a wreath of laurel was hung on the door. Our father taught us that the deceased should be carried out of the house feet first, in order to stop their spirit from looking back, and beckoning for someone else to follow. He knew a great deal about spirits. For instance, when we were ill, he told us that our spirits were wandering, and he would open our bedroom windows, and call out for them to return to us from hills, and forests, and rivers, and vales.

Frannie and I found our mother in the kitchen, cooking lunch. She was chopping potatoes, stirring a pot of vegetable soup. She had untied her hair, which was the color of honey, so it fell over her shoulders and she wore a loose-fitting tunic with a long skirt. I liked this outfit more than her more formal afternoon dresses. She sliced neatly, each vegetable yielding to her precision.

"Did the baby die?" Frannie asked.

Our mother was cutting a carrot, her knife sharp.

"It was stillborn," our mother said.

"Why does that happen?" I asked.

"No way to know, Anne," our mother said.

Steam rose from the soup pot the way fog often rose around our mountain and I watched as our mother diced an onion. She opened an ear of corn, the yellow kernels like teeth; she put a pot of lima beans on the stove for our father, though none of the rest of us liked them.

"Tell your father lunch will be ready soon," our mother said.

Frannie and I found the barn door ajar, the cats asleep on top of the coffins; there were a dozen barn cats, some black with white spots, or white with black spots; one was entirely black and she was my favorite for I met her sometimes in the forest, balanced in the luminous branches of a Clotho tree. Once, she fell from a great height and I watched her arrange herself in midair: the triangles of her ears pointed upward so that she landed neatly on her feet. When Frannie and I entered, the black cat leapt from the coffins and rubbed against our legs, then moved under my hand; she carried an ocean in her throat. We walked to the back room, where our father prepared the dead, and shut the door against the cats.

"Lunch is ready," I said.

Our father was standing in front of his work table, holding the baby in one arm.

"Want to see?" he asked.

Frannie and I crept closer, and he pulled back the blanket to reveal a bald head, an upturned nose, and a tiny, blue mouth. Everything about the baby was closed: the eyes and fists, which rested on either side of the head, and the mouth, which would never open. The baby reminded me of the apples I found in our orchards in fall: soft, bruised, already returning to the earth.

"How would you girls like to help me dig a bucket of peat moss from the bog this afternoon?" our father asked. He went to his desk and lit his pipe.

Frannie and I nodded, soberly, for we were worried by the baby. We knew it belonged to the realm of childhood, as we did, and it reminded us of own deaths, which our mother said were born with us. Our deaths were invisible, but they waited for us in the places where we would meet them: in hallways, or bedrooms, in blizzards or hospitals. Our deaths belonged to some season: winter, when our breath hung, ghostly, in the air, or spring, when our trees turned the newest shade of green, summer when the blossoms grew heavy, and fruit softened, or fall, when the light weakened and our meadow grasses shivered. Our deaths, like our births, belonged to a season, but we did not yet know which one.

"Is the baby a boy or a girl?" Frannie asked at lunch.

"A girl," our mother said.

"Does she have a name?" I asked.

"They were going to call her Lucy," our mother said.

Our mother placed the dead baby in a cradle during lunch, and a breeze drifted through our living room windows, and through our front door, which hung slightly ajar. It filled our curtains like lungs and reminded me of the breaths Lucy refused to take. It occurred to me that Lucy had always belonged to the other world, that she had never opened her eyes, never cried, never used her mouth to drink milk. Lucy was permanently unborn though she had accidentally fallen into this world; she had not seen our September sky, or smelled our rain, or touched the quilts on her parents' bed. She could not walk, so she was learning to be still.

Speck arrived through the crack in our front door, carrying a walnut. He climbed onto the rim of the cradle in which Lucy went on, ignoring the sound of our sipping and chewing; Speck held his nut in both hands, one of his black eyes watching me. After lunch, I carried two buckets, and Frannie carried the shovel, and we followed our father into the forest, like Hansel and Gretel followed their father to the place where he would build fires and leave them alone in the eerie darkness. We walked to the east, where the bog waited; when my mother carried Lucy from our house, back to the barn, I noticed that the baby did not leave our house feet first.

Chapter Two

We had to walk through our Clotho forest to reach the bog and, after a mile, we passed the turrets and dormers of the Scarborough house, which rests on its own dark acres, smoke rising from its chimney. When we moved into our own house, two years before, just after Great Aunt Nora died of pneumonia, the Scarboroughs were the first family to introduce themselves. They warned us that our forest was thick with ghosts; they said there was a ghost woman who hung laundry behind our house at twilight, and a ghost dog who chased wagons at dawn; the mother, Louisa, who bred low, long-nosed hunting dogs and carried a pack of Tarot cards in her skirts, told us the dead slept in the branches of our trees, and washed themselves in Lost River, that they hovered in the mists above our bog; the father, Jasper, who was a logger, and musician, and retired Irish traveller with a caravan still parked in his back yard, told our father about the dead while standing on his porch, with a banjo, or ukulele, or guitar. Our father is half Irish and he and Jasper sat together some Sundays, in our barn, telling stories they learned from their mothers about banshees and changelings; our father smoked a pipe while Jasper breathed a melody into a harmonica.

The Scarboroughs had two auburn-haired daughters, Helen and Josephine, who were thirteen and fifteen, like Frannie and me, and we spent hours in the forest together before they came down with the coughs that left them thin and pale. Helen loved animals of every species, even ugly or fanged or prickly ones, and Josephine loved hats; when they were well, Helen and Josie liked to run with the dachshunds and basset hounds and beagles their mother bred. They liked to play Hide and Seek, and they had a splendid dollhouse in their bedroom, inherited from a grandmother, with miniature bathtubs, and fireplaces, and winding staircases, each room with its own diminutive paintings and rugs. Frannie and I talked about that dollhouse with such excitement that our father built us one of our own; of course Fergus, who makes useful plain furniture and coffins, with doors that close forever, did not understand the delicate nuances of dollhouses, and ours was not detailed or pretty: its doors got stuck and its rooms were all the same rectangular shape: windowless, without the lamps and canopy beds that graced the Scarborough dollhouse. Still, Frannie and I liked fashioning furniture from twigs and string. We liked crocheting rugs and telling stories about a family with a grandfather clock, and a new baby, and a piano; in our stories the piano was haunted and played itself, which frightened the mother and father, but caused the baby to dance. We kept our dollhouse on a table by the window, and

Speck stored nuts in one of the bedrooms, his paws like hands.

I thought of the dead as we passed beneath the dappled shade of the Clotho trees, and I thought of the stories our father read to us at night. Louisa Scarborough said our Clotho forest sprang up after a widowed gypsy burned her late husband's love letters in the acres between our two houses one hundred years before; she said the seeds of the trees came from ashes, and love, and grief.

"What's the peat *for*?" Frannie asked.

"Embalming," our father said.

"Don't you have fluid for that?" I asked.

"Lucy's small," Fergus said.

I didn't know what he meant by this, but I stopped asking questions. Frannie and I knew the smell of the dead when they were not preserved properly. In summer, on our island in North Carolina, we had encountered the high sweet smell of bodies in our grandfather Willem's mortuary, on our way to fishing, or canoeing, or the piece of beach where we buried each other in sand.

At night our father read to us about the Underworld: its gates guarded by a three-headed dog, Cerberus, and the River Styx over which Charon, in his wide hat, ferried the bodies of the deceased, with coins pressed under their tongues, to a world without sunlight or birds. Our father read aloud a story in which a musician named Orpheus married a young girl, Eurydice, and she was bitten by a snake in the meadow of their celebration; Orpheus descended to the Underworld, where the living were not allowed to go, to retrieve his bride. He played a music so beautiful that Cerberus laid down his three heads, and the gates opened wide, and Hades, the God of the Underworld, agreed that Eurydice might return to the living, but only if Orpheus did not turn to look back at her as they passed through the dim subterranean hallways that separate the dead from the living. Orpheus tried to obey, facing forward, until he saw the light at the end of the last dark tunnel, the last cave, and then he did turn, unable to hear Eurydice's footsteps, to be sure she was behind him, and this was when he lost her again: Eurydice floating backwards to that shadowy land of Weeping Willow trees and pomegranate seeds, that place where the dead drink forgetfulness from the River Lethe. Our forest of Clotho trees reminded me of the forest in the Underworld: sunless, thick with vines, flanked by a fast river.

The bog sat at the edge of the forest, in an open, wet place, where a spring fed the earth. Frannie and I looked out at the swaying meadow, which gave way to a bog pool, and a floating mass of moss, on top of wet peat; White Spruce trees grew out of the bog, and Frannie and I liked walking along the surface, our weight causing the trees to sway. Our father was more serious: afraid of darkness, hoping to get home in time for supper. While Frannie and I hopped at the center of the bog, and our father searched for the best place to dig, two bearded men arrived with buckets of their own. Families on our mountain often burned peat for fuel; they shaped it into bricks, and let it dry in their barns, then burned it in their stoves during the narrow days of winter.

"Did you hear about the body?" one of the men asked our father.

"No," Fergus said, motioning for Frannie and me to stay closer; we leapt towards him, from one island of moss to another.

"Jasper found it," the first man said.

The men held their buckets and I saw the outline of the Blue Ridge mountains behind them: shadows of clouds passing over peaks as cold as stone. These were grown men, but they looked small against a mountain range. One of them wore a bowler hat, and the other had a bare head, with a place on top where hair refused to grow.

"Jasper found a girl, wearing a cape," the man with the hat said, "I'd say she was around the same age as your daughters."

"Who is she?" our father asked.

"No one seems to know," the man with the hat said, "no local girls are missing. The cape looks like it could be old, but the body is fresh."

I thought of the girl in the cape and, in my mind, she carried a basket, and spoke with wolves, and hopped from one island of moss to the other, the trees nearby, swaying.

"Finish filling the buckets," our father said, and he went off with the men, to an outcropping of rock, where they sat together. They took pipes from their pockets and, lighting them, began to smoke. Our father likes to talk. In town, where we sometimes went to buy supplies, Frannie and I waited a long time for him to finish his stories, his voice lively in saloons and shops. Our mother complained that Fergus would start a conversation with a lamp post.

"Do you think the girl was from town?" Frannie asked.

"She was from someplace else," I said.

I tried to remember if I had ever owned a cape.

The buckets of peat were heavy, and there was a rainstorm as we retraced our path through the forest. On North Mountain, weather was sudden and fierce; rain fell hard from a stunned sky, or snow began on a gray afternoon, and fell so deeply that our own property became a foreign country; a fog drifted in and, if Frannie and I were playing in the woods, we could not locate the rooftop of our own house. We found ourselves beneath a veil of ignorance, in a place where the world we thought we knew rearranged itself, a place where our own faces and hands were vague. The rain fell hard, then harder, and our father spotted a tree that had not lost its leaves, and sent Frannie and me into the branches so we might have better cover. He stayed below with our buckets, leaned against the trunk. Frannie was a climber, and she ascended more quickly than I did, into that dappled kingdom which belongs to the birds.

"Anne?" Frannie called when she had reached some height that frightened me.

"I don't want to climb that high," I said.

"The branches are sturdy," Frannie said.

"I'm scared," I said.

"Don't look down," Frannie said. I was reminded of how Frannie was drawn to numbers and spiders, her precision and courage like our mother's.

"It's wet," I said, "I might slip."

"You're not afraid of *water*," Frannie said.

This was true: I liked to drift in Lost River, pulled by its current, and looked forward to my baths on Saturdays in the wooden tub our father filled with water he warmed on our stove. I climbed one branch, then another, clinging to the trunk; I could see Frannie's boots above me, in that arboreal cathedral, but I was scared to ascend, and I rested in the low branches, listening to the even beating of the rain.

When we got home, there was a fire flickering in the living room fireplace; Frannie and I changed into dry cotton dresses with cardigans, and set the table, and Louisa had come over, bringing Helen and Josephine. Louisa was wearing a blue afternoon dress; her dresses were expensive, part of an inheritance she brought with her into her marriage—railroad money I heard our parents say. Our mother regarded Louisa's wardrobe with some combination of admiration and envy. Ariel had the sort of face that revealed her feelings; I could tell whether or not she was pleased with me by reading a single crease on her forehead.

"Come over here," our mother said, and she spit on her finger and rubbed some dirt from my cheek.

Our father took the peat to the barn, where I imagined him arranging it around Lucy, and our mother was cooking a chicken, and Louisa was mashing potatoes, and their voices were low, so I knew they were exchanging confidences; Helen wanted to see Speck, who was asleep in his pile of socks on our bed, and Josephine wanted to see our dollhouse, which did not impress her; then, she wanted to see the closet where our mother kept her hats in round boxes. Both Helen and Josie wanted to know if Frannie and I had heard about the girl in the bog.

"Our father found her," Helen said; she fed Speck a peanut from her pocket.

"What does she look like?" Frannie asked.

"She has black hair," Helen said, "like yours Anne, and she's wearing a cape."

"She must be from somewhere else," I said, "not Darkesville."

"Maybe she was out walking alone and she was chased by an animal," Josie said.

We had all been warned against walking quietly in places where we might surprise bears or mountain lions. If we were alone, we carried bells in our pockets or sang.

"What color was the cape?" Frannie asked.

"Do you have a dead baby in your barn?" Helen asked; then she began to cough, for a long time, into the sleeve of her dress. Helen's coughs reminded me of a dog barking.

At dinner, Louisa remembered the Titanic; Frannie and I had read about the sunken ocean liner a few years before, when our father brought home a newspaper, with pictures of the gym, and swimming pool, and Turkish baths, and The Grand Staircase with its oak paneling and bronze angels.

"Some very rich people went down with that ship," Louisa said; she tended to notice money; she wore three rings: one diamond, one ruby, one pearl.

"Jacob Astor," our father said.

"Benjamin Guggenheim," our mother said. "He changed into evening wear, and sat on the deck with his valet, drinking brandy and smoking cigars."

"A true gentleman," our father said.

"They had forty thousand eggs in the kitchen," Frannie said; she loved to count things.

"I wonder what happened to the eggs," I said, "at the bottom of the sea."

"The first class women wore picture hats with ostrich feathers," Josie said.

"There was a cat named Jenny," Helen said, "who ate rats."

Before Josephine and Helen went home, we played Hide and Seek upstairs. I hid my head in my hands, and counted to ten, while Frannie and Josie and Helen ran through the hallways, searching for a clever hiding place; we had played a few times in our house, so I knew to check in the closets and under the bed; I found Frannie on the dark stairs leading to our attic, and Helen was pressed behind the bath-room door, stroking Speck's head, but Josephine, who was often quieter than the rest of us, seemed to have vanished. We hunted for her, lifting and opening and peering into all the familiar places, until her mother called her name, and she rose up from the quilts on my bed: so thin we had overlooked her there, gathering stillness.

That night, while Speck scampered up a chair, and ran along the windowsill, and rain fell steadily on our tin roof, I asked Frannie what she'd heard in the Clotho tree during the storm.

"Something like laughter, or wings," she said, "and words I couldn't understand, as if they were spoken in another language."

"Maybe it was a bird," I said.

There were strange birds in our forest: some huge and gloomy, like something prehistoric, some colorful with strange songs, the sort that lived in the jungles of the stories our father read to us when we sat at our kitchen table with our chalk and slates, going to school—there was a school-house in Martinsburg, just beyond Darkesville, but our parents disapproved of it, so we remained at home.

That night, I dreamed of the Titanic sinking in our bog, only our bog was as deep as the sea. Passengers drowned, then came alive again in their state rooms, where they went on sipping tea from fine china, and playing squash. The men, on their submerged decks, wore smoking jackets and drank bourbon, or gin. In my dream, the Titanic's dead had a second life, a drowned life, that was gentle and slow: their steamer trunks filling with fish, their damp newspapers bringing the same news each day, eggs rolling through their hallways. I dreamed that Bog Girl found herself on The Grand Staircase, in her cape, and she ascended to the dining room, where the chandeliers floated like jellyfish.

Chapter Three

The dead have certain things in common with the trees. I was thinking about this while Frannie and I worked in our mother's garden. Ariel planted nightshades in late spring: tomatoes, potatoes, peppers, and eggplant, all in neat rows, and now we were harvesting them, before the earth grew hard and cold. Frannie and I wore our gardening gloves and old dresses, which were too short. She wore her light hair in braids but I tied mine, full of darkness like our father's, on top of my head. I liked nightshades because they expanded at night, their flowers opening to the moon instead of the sun. While I worked, I watched the Clotho trees, which whitened as their burgundy leaves fainted around them; there was something in the watchful whispering of these trees that reminded me of ghosts. I could feel them observing me, and yet, like the dead, they did not speak. They rose up from the shadows of some other world, their branches filling with song. I wondered what the dead wanted when they returned to the world of the living, for the deceased had no clear beginning, middle, or end. They could not hope to impress anyone with their beauty or wealth.

In summer Louisa liked to frighten Frannie, Helen, Josie, and me on our porch, where we drank iced tea with crushed mint leaves. She liked telling ghost stories. Summer is my favorite season because it is the season of my birth with its long light and blossoms, the season when I tested my mother by entering the world slowly, in a breech position, with a caul over my head; Frannie was an easy birth but I was a hard one. Because our mother and grandmother were midwives Frannie and I already knew the language of birth with its broken waters and contractions. We knew what our arrivals suggested about us: Frannie's easy good fortune and my own murkier destiny. Louisa told us ghost children travelled alone on roads, and that they smelled like lavender; she said ghosts walked up staircases, again and again, carrying lanterns because they were looking for something lost, something that could never be found. She said ghosts were ruled by seasons and tides. Louisa told us ghosts knocked on doors, and made rooms cold, that they banged pots and pans, and caused handprints to appear on mirrors. There was one who died before her wedding who made her wedding dress dance. She said ghosts stood in windows, gazing out at the vanished acres of the past; Frannie and I believed her stories, and the stories of our other neighbors, who said there were underground caves through which the dead returned to North Mountain. They said the dead slid into the branches of night, and drank from Lost River, remembering their mortal thirst; the dead liked the way our breath became smoke in winter; they enjoyed snow, because it shimmered, and they could shape it into furniture and gowns. They liked the way the drifts were rearranged by the wind. Frannie thought a ghost lived in our closet, which was overgrown with scraps of fabric we had not yet sewn into a quilt; she said she could see the outline of a sleeping girl sometimes at dusk, among the squares of cloth.

Our mother was away, delivering a baby for a big-boned woman, Mrs. Davidson, who lived on a farm and already had five kids, all of them with freckles, and our father was in the forest, cutting down a Clotho tree; he had been using pine coffins ever since we arrived, shipped by train from our old life in North Carolina, but now he needed a tiny white coffin for Lucy, whose funeral would take place tomorrow; I could hear his axe, chopping, and the sound of hooves. A wagon arrived in our driveway and a man in a brown suit and hat called out.

"Your father home?" he asked.

"In the forest," I said.

I could see something draped in the back of his wagon, and the man with the hat nodded before disappearing into the leafy shadows. His horses' ears twitched; they swatted flies with their tails. We waited until we could not hear the man walking through the leaves anymore; then, Frannie and I lifted the sheet in the back of the wagon, and this is when we first saw Bog Girl: her black hair braided like ours, her skin tanned from soaking in peat, her cape blue. She was our size, and might have been our sister: the wild one our mother forgot to have, the one who would have climbed the highest trees, higher even than Frannie; she would have been a faster swimmer than I was, diving deeper into eddies, and she would have asked to play Briar Rose, or the eldest dancing princess, when we enacted our fairy tales.

In the story of the dancing princesses, Frannie and I pretended to be all twelve princesses, and, in that fairy tale, we had a bedroom floor that descended to another world, where boats floated us across a lake, to a castle, where we could not stop dancing. We fell in love with a marble ballroom in a hidden kingdom, and, each night, we danced until we tore holes in our shoes; this was among my favorite fairy tales, and sometimes Helen and Josie performed it with us. We all wore white nightgowns, and took down our hair, and danced; Helen danced with a cat in her arms, her face buried in its fur, and Josie danced without making a sound in a big Merry Widow hat that had been discarded by Louisa, and Frannie danced a tidy, precise waltz she had been taught by our father, and I danced ecstatically with my arms in the air, whirling; in the tale we danced all night, never sleeping, until we were thin and tired, and our father, the King, did not understand why we could not sleep, and we did not tell him about our other life, beneath the floorboards, across a lake, where the music beckoned.

Frannie and I would have to can the tomatoes and peppers, which I lined up on the kitchen counter, and we would eat most of the eggplant, quickly, but keep the potatoes in the cellar in a patch of cool earth; I did not look forward to these things. The living are hungry, and we want things -- dresses, furniture, copper pots -- but Bog Girl, sunk in her tub of earth, had no interest in ribbons or jewelry. Her hands were empty; she seemed to want nothing.

Our father and the man in the suit slipped out of the forest and stood behind the wagon; it seemed to me that our forest had doors, made of the shadows between the trees, through which we all came and went. Frannie and I saw the two of them lift Bog Girl, carefully, and carry her into our barn. At dinner, we ate ham sandwiches, and our mother still wasn't home. Our father left us to do the dishes; he returned to the barn, where he was carving two white coffins from Clotho trees; he had agreed to keep Bog Girl on display in our barn, during the funeral for Lucy, in the hopes that someone might recognize her. If no one did, she would be buried, like Lucy, in the cemetery beside the Methodist church, where the gates are made of iron, and wealthy families sleep together in marble mausoleums. Frannie and I looked at the clock on the mantle and knew we would have to clean and prepare the front parlor without our mother, for she was still several miles away, waiting for Mrs. Davidson's baby.

The next day, Lucy's parents, The Mallicoats, and their neighbors, and congregation, would come to our parlor and gaze at Lucy, resting in her white Clotho coffin: Lucy, who was never hungry, and could not roll over in bed, or lie, or go crazy, or bake a pie. Before the mourners arrived, Frannie and I went into the forest to gather the white flowers we placed around Lucy's head, and on our mantle, above the fireplace, where flames seemed alive like waves in the sea. These flowers grew out of the Clotho trees themselves, curving like pipes. Louisa called them ghost plants or Ghost Pipes; they were pale flowers that did not rise from the ground, flowers that drank gloom instead of light.

Lucy's parents, the Mallicoats, were young farmers, and Lucy was their first and only child. They wanted to take her home with them, and hold her, to feed her applesauce, and teach her the names of the world's objects. The Mallicoats missed who Lucy might have been, so their grief was different from the families who mourned the old, or half grown; they had not known Lucy; they had imagined her. At the funeral, Mrs. Mallicoat cut off a lock of Lucy's hair so that she might place it in a shadow box; she was wearing the black bombazine dress she would go on wearing for a year. Her husband, Jack, thin with a mustache, fiddled with a pocket watch and kept his hands in the pockets of his only suit. A wide church lady with a monocle and short, tightly curled hair played piano, and our kitchen table was laid with food: potato salad, chicken, lima beans, blackberry pie.

Frannie and I were supposed to clean and keep quiet. Our father, who had grown up learning the business of funerals, showed us how it was done. He had met our mother at a funeral for her drowned brother, Liam, when they were both fourteen; they kissed for the first time in a cemetery where the tombs were above ground because the sea was forever rising. Fergus explained that a funeral was for the living, not the dead. He told us about the ancient Egyptian mummies, with their brains and hearts and livers in canopic jars, their bodies wrapped in linens and salt, their tombs full of objects they would need in the afterlife: boats, chariots, chairs. He told us about Avalon, where King Arthur was taken on a golden bed after he was fatally wounded in battle: a place beyond mists where apples grew year round, and Arthur's sister, a witch, watched over him, the island keeping him alive so he might return someday to save his troubled kingdom. Our father taught us to arrange the flowers (Frannie's arrangements were always more pleasing than my own) and serve the food. He told us about the ancient alchemists who hoped to forge a stone that would heal all forms of illness, and grant eternal life, a stone that would cause common crystals to transform into diamonds; he reminded us of the three Greek Spinners who controlled the destinies of mortals: Clotho, who spins the thread of life, Lachesis, who determines the length, and Atropos, who cuts the thread when the time has come for our deaths. In spring he advised Frannie and me to tell our secrets to the bees, who lived in a wax castle with a fat queen, and we did this, when we came across a hive in the woods or a neighbor's yard: leaned close and whispered.

Our mother came home in the middle of the funeral: her face tired, her green eyes shining, her fine golden hair tied on top of her head in its familiar knot. She shook hands with the Mallicoats, and led them to the barn where she gave them a grief doll she had been sewing. The doll resembled Lucy, with an upturned nose and tiny fists, and Mrs. Mallicoat took it in her arms; Frannie and I could see that Mrs. Mallicoat's arms had been empty. Our father ushered the rest of the funeral party into the barn, and opened the white Clotho coffin, where Bog Girl, packed in peat, went on napping in her cape. The tone of the funeral shifted, since Bog Girl was unknown: a stranger with dark braids, who died in our forest; Bog Girl was a mystery, instead of a source of grief:

like Rip Van Winkle when he woke on his hillside, in the Catskill Mountains, with an endless beard, twenty years after drinking with ghosts, his dog, Wolf, long gone, his nagging wife finally silent. Bog Girl was a mystery like the sleeping girls in our fairy tales: Snow White with the poison apple of jealousy caught in her throat, Sleeping Beauty whose entire kingdom slumbered with her for a century after she pricked her finger on a curse.

"She looks like your daughters," Mrs. Mallicoat said to our mother, who came over with a frowning mouth to see.

"She could be their sister," Mr. Mallicoat agreed.

"Or cousin," the wide church lady offered.

"Is that a squirrel?" a child with long eyelashes asked Frannie.

Speck had climbed the side of the coffin without us noticing, because we were busy staring into the face of Bog Girl; he began orbiting the rim, his tail wild.

"That's our pet, Speck," I said.

"Speck?" the church lady asked.

"Because he's small," Frannie said, "like a speck of dust."

"I have a fox," the child said, "it's red and sleeps on my porch."

"The fox is wild," the child's mother said.

Our procession moved beside Lost River; Frannie and I could hear this river through our open bedroom windows in spring, when the snow melted and the water swelled, outgrowing its banks. Lost River had waterfalls where canoes capsized and were swallowed by rapids. It was where I leapt from the high cliffs in summer and was carried to a hanging cave; it was a place where wagons and horses were swallowed by swift currents. Our father said it was like the River Lethe in the Underworld, from which the dead drank forgetfulness: the lives they once lived forgotten. Lost River flowed through caves and canyons; in fall, the salmon spawned and we could see them, leaping towards their deaths.

Our procession moved in wagons, towards the village cemetery, which sleeps behind an iron fence, beside a white clapboard church, where our family does not sing or sit in pews. There are three churches in Darkesville: one Catholic, one Baptist, one Methodist; the clapboard one is Methodist. We Van Beests are agnostic; we have a Bible in our house and our father has read passages to Frannie and me, so we might know about when to mourn and when to dance, and about Adam and Eve standing naked in their garden, and their Tree of Knowledge heavy with fruit, and Noah's ark, with its pairs of animals, riding through the flood to Mount Ararat. Frannie and I were instructed by our father to tell the villagers: *We go to school and practice religion at home*. It mattered that we were liked because we wanted the neighbors to trust us with their babies and their dead. Fergus believed in science, and myths, and fairy tales, and Ariel was a spiritualist, who favored seances where she spoke to her dead sister and brother: one drowned before he could grow up, the other washed away by grief. The Scarboroughs were descended on Jasper's side from a long line of gypsy travellers; they were lapsed Catholics whose true religion lay in distances and caravans, in tea leaves and Tarot cards, so we knew their secrets, and they came to know ours. We knew, for instance, that

Jasper was more in love with Louisa than she was with him, that her family had money and lived in a mountain town his caravan passed through each year of his youth. We knew that Jasper had pursued Louisa with love letters and gifts, that she had to have pretty things in order to be kept happy, and that keeping her happy was not easy; we saw Jasper sitting in a rocking chair alone on their front porch some evenings, rocking fast and hard, his worry like a ship in a storm.

In the cemetery we gathered beside two holes in the ground, beneath a white tent, and as the minister spoke of the innocence and purity of babies, thunder rumbled; when he held his hands towards the sky, to ask that the Lord bless Mr. and Mrs. Mallicoat in their hour of need, raindrops fell. Lucy was under our tent, in her tiny white coffin, unaware of the way the wind began to blow from the east. I could see her expressionless face from the chairs where Frannie and I grew restless, our hands folding and unfolding; I was dreaming of chicken pot pie. I thought of the future: the furniture Frannie and I would build for our dollhouse, and the stories our father would read to us once our fire was lit and our windows blackened.

There was a second tent, across the cemetery, where Bog Girl had no mourners, and went on dreaming of her bog, with its floating islands and shivering trees. At the end of the service, it was decided by the minister, and sexton, and gravediggers, that the burials of both bodies would take place in the morning. The mourners went home, through the white forest, riding beside Lost River, the air growing cold. There was a cellar beneath the church

Chapter Four

None of us were prepared for what the grave-diggers found in the morning. We had heard stories of people with a certain sleeping sickness who awakened at their own funerals, or worse, found themselves knocking on buried doors: people who seemed dead, but were not. There were stories of changelings: human babies replaced with white-haired fairy babies who screamed and spit. In our book of Greek Myths, a girl named Persephone lived half her life in the Underworld, as the wife of Hades, the God of the dead, and half among the living, where she walked in golden fields with her mother, drinking sunlight.

The sky had just turned pink when two gravediggers descended to the cellar to retrieve Lucy and Bog Girl. The gravediggers heard something—a singing, or a kind of muted whining—and they lifted their lanterns, expecting to find a raccoon. Instead, they discovered Lucy, sitting up, sucking her own fingers, the wreath of Ghost Pipe still woven into her hair. She was in the coffin of Bog

Girl, who was also upright, holding Lucy in her lap. The gravediggers were so frightened they dropped their lanterns, and one shattered, its flame beneath the bottom stair, which began to smolder, and Bog Girl screamed. This scream attracted the minister, and his wife, who fetched a bucket of water; the minister's wife saw smoke, and thought the trouble was fire; then, the gravediggers emerged from the depths, with peat on their shirts and faces, one holding Lucy against his chest, the other carrying Bog Girl as a new husband might carry a bride. Lucy waved at the minister and his wife, her tiny hand opening and closing, and the minister, George, fainted in front of his own office, where he wrote his sermons, while his wife, Edna, ran into the rectory to search for wine. This would all be written down many times: first, in our Darkesville newspaper, then again in the newspapers of cities like New York and Chicago. Over and over, the gravediggers would drop their lanterns, and the minister would faint, while his wife twisted a corkscrew. There was a scientific investigation, and one carried out by detectives from distant cities; our father was interviewed about how, exactly, he packed the bodies in peat, and where he got the coffins. Our mother was interviewed about Lucy's birth, in our parlor, while Frannie and I pressed our ears to holes in the upstairs floorboards.

"You're sure the child was *stillborn*?" We heard a man with a beard and notebook ask.

"She did not breathe," our mother said.

Then, outside, the wind began to blow: the forest leaning, our father pulling hard at the barn door.

Frannie and I saw Lucy and Bog Girl alive for the first time in the graveyard the day they awakened. They were being given milk by the minister's wife and were huddled together, beneath a Clotho tree, at the edge of the forest, where they were wrapped in blankets. Their eyes seemed troubled by so much light.

"It's a miracle," I heard the minister's wife say.

Mr. and Mrs. Mallicoat had been summoned from the village, and they stood a few feet from the place where two holes had been dug just the day before, the earth still open to receive their daughter, who now blinked and drank from a tin cup.

"Jesus showed us this was possible," the minister said. He was a vain man, I think, excited by his sudden fame; he recovered from his faint once his wife offered him a gulp of wine.

Already, the gravediggers had returned to their cabins and cottages to change their clothes, and they told their stories to their families: how two of the dead had come back from their stiff silence to rejoin the living, how the bodies they were preparing to bury, through some alchemy, had returned to us. People believed or they did not believe; they thought of themselves, of their own feeble family members, and asked how such a thing had happened; they wondered if it might happen again. Our forest was known for its supernatural qualities so the oldest locals, like the blacksmith and the hatter, said they were not the least bit surprised. They said the dead had returned to Darkesville during the time of their great-grandmothers, stepping out of the forest and caves the way we stepped out of our bedrooms in the morning. They said they had always known the dead would return again.

In the graveyard, the Mallicoats approached Lucy slowly, as if she might be a feral animal. Mr. Mallicoat touched Lucy's wild hair, and Mrs. Mallicoat offered Lucy a finger, which she held in her tiny fist. They had brought a quilt from home, and they wrapped Lucy in it. Lucy did not cry and she did not smile; she said later that she found the faces of her parents both strange and familiar. Then, the Mallicoats climbed into their wagon, and drove through town, and Mrs. Mallicoat held her baby in her lap. The residents of Darkesville came to their windows, and stood on their porches, watching.

Bog Girl was alone now, wrapped in a blanket, with her cup of milk, and she trembled. The minister and his wife offered to keep her: the minister, George, must have imagined his fame increasing with each newspaper reporter, each interview. But the minister's wife, Edna, was afraid of children, having been barren for so many years that she had fallen in love with order and silence. (My mother said the sight of Bog Girl, who had been soaked in peat, filled Edna with dismay.) So, when our parents offered to take Bog Girl home with us, and care for her until other arrangements could be made, Edna persuaded her husband that this would be for the best.

"They have girls of their own," she said. "They know what she needs."

"I will visit," the minister agreed, "and offer counsel."

"Lovely idea," his wife said, and you could almost *see* her thinking of her immaculate bedroom, with its iron bed and polished floor, of her shiny sink and knives, her fine china in which her round face was reflected.

Chapter Five

Frannie and I were excited and frightened by Bog Girl. She was like a new sister, but she was also a recently deceased stranger. I wondered, for example, if she would enjoy needlepoint like Frannie or swimming like me. Our parents seemed confused too because, when we got home, our father went directly to the barn to build a simple bed frame for Bog Girl, so she would not have to sleep with Frannie and me, while our mother warmed water on the stove for a bath. Bog Girl sat in front of our fireplace, in a rocking chair, wrapped in a blanket and her teeth chattered; she could not seem to get warm.

"Make her a pot of tea, girls," our mother said, and when we went into the kitchen, to light the stove, Bog Girl followed us with her eyes, which were the color of licorice.

There was a knock on the door and Louisa arrived with Helen and Josie, in new wool coats; they had seen our wagon from a distance, moving through the forest, with a strange girl seated between Frannie and me. They had already heard that Bog Girl had risen from the chilled earth beneath the church. Josie and Helen came into our kitchen, pulling off their sweaters; Josie was wearing a new Gainsborough chapeau.

"I like your hat," I said.

"My grandmother sent it to me," Josie said. Her auburn hair was piled high beneath the brim.

Louisa and our mother went to fetch a wooden tub for a bath. Bog Girl continued rocking, in front of our fireplace, her face luminous.

"Does she speak?" Josie asked.

"Not yet," I said.

"Maybe she speaks another language, like French," Helen suggested. She reached her hand down to touch our black cat.

"Do you think she could tell us what it's like to be dead?" Josie asked.

"We're supposed to help her get warm," Frannie said.

"I'm making a pot of tea," I said.

"We should feed her," Helen said.

"I know how to fry potatoes," I said.

The potatoes were in the cellar; Josie and I carried them upstairs in our skirts; I sliced them inexactly with our mother's sharpest knife, and arranged them in the iron frying pan where they began to sizzle.

"Shall I serve her tea?" Helen asked.

She poured a cup and walked towards Bog Girl, the cup rattling in the saucer; we watched the silhouette of Helen, thin from coughing, holding the cup out to Bog Girl, who would not reach for it.

"Maybe she doesn't know what to do," Josie said. She spoke quietly, one of her hands twisting a strand of her long auburn hair.

"She was drinking milk from a cup this afternoon," I said.

"Let's *all* have tea," Frannie said, pouring out four more cups that steamed on the kitchen table; Frannie and Josie and I lifted our cups to sip, demonstrating how it might be done, and Helen held Bog Girl's out again, the cup rattling against the saucer.

"Maybe she doesn't like tea," I said.

"Who doesn't like *tea?*" Helen said.

"Let's try warm milk," I said.

Frannie went to our ice box and returned with a glass bottle, which had been delivered in the early morning by our milkman. The milk looked bluish white in the firelit dusk; she poured it into a pot, and stirred it with a wooden spoon. Then, she flipped over my potatoes with a fork; I had already forgotten the potatoes, which is the sort of cook I would grow up to be: my toast burned at breakfast, my chicken boiled until it was rubbery, my carrots wizened, my mind on something else. Frannie poured the milk in a cup, and Helen held it out. This time Bog Girl's hand darted out from under the blankets to receive it. We watched her sip, and tried to think of something to say.

"Have you heard of the Titanic?" I asked.

"Why are you asking her about *that?*" Frannie said.

"It was in the news," I said.

"Where did you come from?" Helen asked.

Bog Girl looked at Helen, steadily, and took another sip of milk.

"Is someone cooking potatoes?" our mother asked when she and Louisa returned.

"I am," I said.

"Bog Girl won't speak," Helen said.

"She *was* dead yesterday," Frannie said.

Our mother slid the potatoes onto a plate and left them steaming on the kitchen table.

"Louisa and I are going to give Bog Girl a bath," our mother said.

"Do you think Bog Girl has heard of the Titanic?" I asked.

"It may take her a while to remember things," Louisa said.

"She's not going to let you bathe her," Josie said.

"What if water isn't good for her?" I said.

"Water is good for *everyone*," our mother said.

"Moon," Bog Girl said, standing up and looking out the window, her blanket falling away so her blue cape fluttered behind her.

"What did she say?" Frannie asked.

"Is she speaking French?" Helen asked.

Then, Bog Girl walked to the kitchen table and began eating potatoes, with her hands.

"I'm going to have to teach her manners," Frannie said.

Our father knocked on the front door and, when I opened it, he carried his twin bed frame into the living room, and placed it in front of the fire; he had fashioned a headboard, footboard, and slats from the remains of a Clotho tree; the bed glowed in the firelight, its frame as white as bones.

"She's eating," our father said.

Bog Girl said nothing, her mouth full.

"I need some help in the barn, stuffing a mattress," our father said.

"I'll help," Frannie said.

"Fergus, can you bring in the tub?" our mother said.

When our father went out, the black barn cat leapt on top of Bog Girl's chair.

"Gossamer," Bog Girl said, and the black cat, whose whiskers were as fine as spider's silk, and whose velvet ears and eyes were as dark as soot, slipped into her lap.

There are so many ways to die. Helen, who felt she would die young, kept a list in her journal which was decorated with sketches of animals: sheep, chickens, foxes, starlings. Frannie and I kept journals too; Frannie's was neat, her handwriting a series of careful loops and curls, her entries daily, while mine was a sprawling untended mess.

"An Athenian lawmaker was smothered by gifts of cloaks, showered on him in a theatre," Helen said.

"He died of cloaks?" I asked.

"He was *smothered*," Frannie corrected.

We were sharing our bed so Louisa and our mother could keep vigil downstairs, near Bog Girl. When he arrived through our window, in early evening, Speck did not sleep with Helen, Josie, Frannie and me; he found an open sock drawer, tucked his nose into his tail, and became a circle of stillness.

"A man in Austria died when he broke his neck after tripping over his own beard," Helen said.

"Why didn't he trim his beard?" Josie asked.

"A French composer died of an infected sore, after accidentally piercing his foot with a staff, while conducting a symphony," Helen said.

"These people are *ridiculous*," Josephine said.

"I bet there are people who have been killed by hats," Helen said.

"Hats make everyone happy," Josie said.

I heard the stairs creak and Fergus appeared in our doorway. "How about a story?" he asked as he settled into the deep chair by the window, opening our book of Grimm fairy tales; he began reading the one about a girl in a cape, Red Riding Hood, delivering a basket of cake and wine to her sick grandmother. She was traveling alone, through the woods, when she met a wolf; the wolf asked where she was going, and Red Riding Hood told him about her grandmother's cottage. The wolf hurried there, while Red Riding Hood was picking flowers; he swallowed the grandmother whole, dressed himself in her nightgown and hat. When Red Riding Hood arrived at the cottage she noticed her grandmother, in bed, looking strange.

"How could she not see that the wolf was wearing her grandmother's clothes?" Josie asked.

"The grandmother was sick, so she expected her to look different," Helen said.

"But a sick grandmother wouldn't have looked *hairy*," Frannie said.

"What big ears you have," our father read.

"All the better to hear you with," I said.

"What big eyes you have," our father read.

"All the better to see you with," Frannie said.

Chapter Six

For a moment, our town was famous, and we were famous. People came from far away, some driving Model T cars instead of horses; they came to speak to Jasper Scarborough about how he discovered Bog Girl and what it was like to pull her from the peat.

"She'd risen to the surface," Jasper said, "I could see her nose."

A man with a beard and a deep voice interviewed the Mallicoats and our mother about the details of Lucy's birth. (Was she *really* stillborn or had she been just *a little bit* alive?) He interviewed the gravediggers, and the minister and his wife, who spoke of miracles. In Darkesville, people became convinced that our father could raise the dead, that if he could preserve bodies with peat and other secret ingredients, exactly as he had with Lucy and Bog Girl, the dead of our village would return to us; they would open their eyes, and step out of death as Red Riding Hood and her grandmother had stepped out of the belly of the wolf when a huntsman cut them free, his axe opening the hot pall.

In the morning, we found Bog Girl asleep beside the fireplace, in the bed our father built for her. She was holding the black cat she would always call Gossamer. Our mother and Louisa had slept upright in rocking chairs, because they had been worried about Bog Girl running away: back to her bog maybe, or into the deep recesses of the forest which were thick with ghosts and caves and vines. Louisa had managed to scrub Bog Girl, and her hair was freshly braided. Her skin was still tanned from the bog and she was wearing a nightgown instead of her cape, which had been washed and hung to dry on our front porch, its thick blue fabric billowing in the wind.

The Mallicoats came to breakfast and brought Lucy, who wore a white christening dress and travelled in a perambulator. My mother and father began cooking: coffee, pancakes, fried potatoes, blackberry pie; Frannie, Josephine, Helen and I set the table; Helen and Josephine argued about the correct placement of dessert spoons.

"Above the dinner plate," Josie said.

"Beside the other spoon," Helen said.

Louisa raised her eyebrows.

When the Mallicoats arrived Beatrice Mallicoat held Lucy in her arms, but soon Lucy made a high screeching sound and reached her arms towards the bed, where Bog Girl was warming herself beside the fire. Beatrice settled Lucy beside Bog Girl, who patted the baby on the head, and they ate their breakfasts together, on a quilt with the cat, the two of them sitting with their backs close to the fire because they could not seem to get warm. Bog Girl and Lucy ate potatoes and drank milk. (Lucy sucked her potatoes instead of chewing them.) They did not touch the pancakes drenched in maple syrup; they refused the coffee with its sugar and heavy cream. On this day, Bog Girl and Lucy were still mysterious to us; we had not yet learned that they preferred to eat night-shades from Ariel's garden, because food grown in darkness is the food of the recently dead. We did not know that they would always crave milk with honey or that their eyes were troubled by light; we did not yet realize that neither of them would grow or age as we did, that they would always suffer from a slight chill, even in summer. We wanted them to tell us about death, about what they could remember of that valley on the other side, but they preferred to climb our trees and speak to the birds. They were drawn to Lost River, which they could hear in spring, when the snow on North Mountain began to melt; they were drawn to underground caves we could not detect. We did not yet know they could see the future, like Merlin in my book of Arthurian myths, who could name the knights that would sit at Camelot's round table, even before they were born. Frannie brought down our dollhouse after breakfast and placed it near the hearth. Bog Girl and Lucy liked arranging its furniture together while Helen, Josephine, and I washed dishes, our hands deep in suds.

"Did you live in a house like this?" Frannie asked Bog Girl.

"I don't know," Bog Girl said.

In my imagination, Bog Girl was born from the bog, the peat like a womb. In Darkesville it was believed that Bog Girl's family came from Penn-sylvania or Ohio, that they probably lost her while crossing Lost River in spring, when it is most swol-len, or perhaps in the Clotho forest at dusk. For a while our sheriff sent pictures of Bog Girl to nearby towns and cities: her green eyes squinting, her black hair in braids, her cape, which she continued to wear no matter what other coats and sweaters we offered, levitating behind her in the breeze.

Later that week, Lucy and Bog Girl would be inspected by our doctor, Fred Saunders, who would notice their body temperatures hovered five degrees below our own, and their pupils were permanently dilated, as if they were always peering into night. He would notice that Lucy was acquiring language and mobility at a startling rate. He tested Bog Girl's memory of the past and found she possessed only images and fragments, her time in the bog, and her days before like the hull of a broken ship settling to the bottom of the sea. I thought of Bog Girl deep in the moss and peat, her cape around her, the White Spruces filling with snow or birds. But this was the first day, before we knew Lucy would come to our house on many afternoons, before we knew our father would acquire so much funeral business he would have to hire help, before Helen grew thinner and her cheeks flushed. It was before the villagers and newspapers decided Lucy and Bog Girl had been a hoax, that they were children who pretended to return from the dead for fame or fortune.

We went out on the porch and Frannie showed Lucy and Bog Girl how to jump rope; I told the story of Goldilocks and the Three Bears and Bog Girl listened intently; when Goldilocks stepped out of the forest into a house that did not belong to her, I saw Bog Girl tilt her head to one side; when Goldilocks tried out all the bowls of porridge, and lay down in all the beds, preferring the smallest one, Bog Girl smiled a little, her front teeth as white as the Clotho trees. This was before I knew that Bog Girl's favorite book would be *The Jungle Book*, in which a human boy was raised by animals, that she would carry it to bed with her, after she remembered how to read, and examine the sketches of a half-naked child swinging on vines. Even then, Bog Girl and Lucy watched Speck leap out our bedroom window and disappear into the branches of the forest, their eyes following his flight.

brushes to comb their hair. It was not clear why the dead congregated on North Mountain, or what they wanted when they returned through our caves, or spoke to us in the canopies of our Clotho forest. The living regarded the dead with anxiety and curiosity, but the dead did not reveal their thoughts about us; we did not know why they came; we did not know when, or if, they would go.

Helen was being sent away to a sanatorium because her consumption had worsened. Two corpses arrived in our barn with the expectation that our father was now able to raise the dead. Our mother was delivering fewer babes than usual. Certain pregnant women were spooked by the story of Lucy; they wondered if our mother could tell a living child from a dead one, if she would fake the deaths of babies so her husband could grow famous resurrecting them. Our mother competed with one hospital, fifty miles away, and with a young woman named Rose who had recently learned midwifery from her grandmother. When our mother said Rose's name she sounded as if she had swallowed vinegar. Our father used to tell us his main competition was the natural thrift that led some West Virginians to bury their dead on their own land; this was one difference we all noticed between the citizens of North Carolina and the citizens of our mountain: in North Carolina hats, lawns, and garden parties followed strict rules while, here in West Virginia, what mattered most to citizens and animals was *freedom*. It had been hard when we first arrived from North Carolina for our parents to earn the trust of our new neighbors. They had relied on Great Aunt Nora's best friend, a busty florist named Phoebe, who always had a carnation pinned to her dress, to introduce them, and help them acquire their first pregnant ladies and corpses. Then, that first spring, Phoebe died of a heart attack while shoveling snow, her body delivered to my father by the boy who brought her newspaper, and my parents waited to see if word of their skills would spread without a local emissary. We had moved because our father was Great Aunt Nora's favorite nephew, and she was childless, and he had inherited her property, but we would have to pack up and return to our hot island in North Carolina if there was not enough work.

In those first weeks, after Lucy and Bog Girl stepped out of their coffins, Frannie and I found ourselves competing for Bog Girl's attention. Frannie taught her to climb trees while I read her stories. Frannie gave her a dress and I offered her a pair of stockings. Frannie showed Bog Girl how to count, and I showed her how to add just enough honey to her milk. We both showed her how to arrange the furniture in our dollhouse and rule over its miniature domestic dramas. I dreamed that Bog Girl told me her secrets; I dreamed Bog Girl and I were floating through the sunken hallways of the Titanic together and she introduced me to each drowned passenger: levitating in their heavy, wet staterooms, their teacups full of barnacles, their shoes filling with minnows. I wanted Bog Girl to like me *more* than Frannie but, after a while, I saw her only real family was Lucy; they had been born together in that cold, windowless cellar beneath the Methodist Church and they understood one another in the wordless way that family members often do. Bog Girl may have looked like me but she was not my sister.

Lucy's mother, Beatrice, noticed that Lucy cried and was listless if she could not spend time with Bog Girl, so Frannie, Bog Girl, and I babysat for Lucy most afternoons. On the day of the first snowfall Frannie and I had taken Bog Girl and Lucy onto the front lawn to show them how to build a snowman. We wrapped them in scarves and mittens, and still they shivered at the edge of the Clotho forest, their faces upturned so they could watch the immaculate flakes fall; I could tell they found the snow pleasing by the way they surveyed it, and dropped it into their pockets. The day slanted and drifted, our acres growing soft.

We could hear Fergus in the barn, hammering coffins; he was preserving two dead bodies: an old woman with long silver hair who fell down a flight of stairs, and a middle-aged man who ate a plate of sausages, and complained of an ache under his ribs, before lowering himself into bed and never rising again. These were our father's first bodies since Lucy and Bog Girl and he was trying to remember what steps he followed to bring about miracles. He cut down more Clotho trees for their coffins, went by wagon to gather peat from the bog. Frannie and I were demonstrating how to roll a snowball; we gathered snow in our mittened hands and shaped it into a circle, then rolled it, end over end, through the gathering white. This excited Bog Girl, who came over to help us push the snowball uphill, towards the barn, while Lucy wandered on short, stout legs to the place where the barn door hung open, our father hammering. In the back room of the barn, Lucy was drawn to the dead bodies with their expressionless faces and stiff arms. She climbed into a coffin to sit with the old woman and hold her hand: snow fell trees. I liked the crunch my feet made in the gathering snow, and the path I made walking from the house, across the yard; I liked parting the branches of the Clotho trees which were now as heavy and white as clouds. The forest, lost in its blizzard, might have been a room in heaven: marble statues, vaulted ceiling, a floor made of ivory. I laid down my basket and dug along the base of my favorite grove of trees, the ones Frannie and I climbed when we finished enacting our fairy tales: jealous stepmothers speaking with their mirrors, spinning wheels burning at the center of town, a pregnant woman eating lettuce from a witch's garden. I thought of Frannie climbing higher and higher up the ladder of branches, the world growing small beneath her. I was digging at the base of my third tree, my breath ethereal, when I found a bit of wilted Ghost Pipe and, pulling it away from the trunk, I heard something shifting above me, in the canopy. I turned my face upward, snow falling in my eyes, and heard someone call my name; I heard wings. In the book of Greek myths our father read to us, beside our window, his lantern's flame like a tongue, I learned that death was one of the children of night: a bearded and winged man, and I felt he was up there, watching me gather Ghost Pipe in a basket while, inside, the dead warmed themselves beside our fire, their cups of milk half empty; then, a branch shook and our black cat, Gossamer, landed beside me: snow between his ears, his tail tall. He followed me into the yard, and we turned towards the barn together, where my father was still leaned over his dream of resurrection, arranging the old woman and the middle-aged man just as he had arranged Bog Girl and Lucy.

"I found the flowers," I said.

"We'll have to store these bodies under the church for one night," my father said, "so everything is the same."

"It rained the day we tried to bury Lucy," I reminded him.

"I'll hire the rainmaker," my father said. "Do you want a bite of chocolate?"

I nodded and we walked to the far corner of his work room, stopping to wash our hands in a bucket. Fergus had a desk back there, without breezes or cats, beyond the strange paintings and moth-eaten furniture Great Aunt Nora had left behind, buried in hay. In the highest locked drawer of that desk, he kept a dozen chocolate bars and I would find him, when he was worried or tired, standing in front of that desk, chewing slowly. Fergus was usually light-hearted but this task of trying to resurrect the dead had made him tense. I could see it in his tightened jaw, and in the way he tore open the wrappers of his chocolate bars, and in the embers of his pipe. I thought of the rainmaker, Benjamin McCoy, who came from a nearby town each time our farmers endured a drought, and stood at the top of a wooden platform, stirring his secret mixture of twenty-three chemicals in galvanized tanks, the air around him acrid with magic.

When I returned to the house I found our mother making a pot of Brunswick stew, Helen and Frannie sewing a quilt at the kitchen table, and Louisa with her pack of Tarot cards. Bog Girl and Lucy sat on Bog Girl's bed, the fire at their backs.

"Want a cup of stew?" my mother asked, when I came inside, and closed the door, the white world disappearing behind me; Josie was leaned over our piano, playing the songs in our music books: *Ave Maria* and *All Things Bright and Beautiful*. I put down my basket of flowers and walked to the kitchen table, where Helen's future was arranged in the shape of a Celtic Cross. Louisa had brown eyes and auburn hair and long fingers and she kept her cards wrapped in a purple scarf; she had learned to read futures from Jasper's mother, when she was very young, and in this light it was easy to see why Jasper had written love letters for a year until she agreed to court him; I could see that one of the cards showed a fool stepping off a cliff, and one had the image of a ship leaving port; there was a card on which a chariot was pulled by winged horses; I could see a bolt of lightning, and a card depicting a broken door.

"This card means you'll take a long journey," Louisa said.

"A train ride," Helen agreed.

"This one, here, says you'll begin in a state of innocence," Louisa said, "while this one suggests you will make an important discovery."

"What does a sanatorium look like?" Frannie asked.

"This one is at a high elevation," Louisa said, "where the air is cold and clean."

"Helen will sit on the veranda," Bog Girl said, "even when it snows."

"This card," Louisa said, "shows that you will enjoy nature."

"Helen will meet a man who limps and wears glasses," Bog Girl said.

"I should get *you* a deck of cards," Louisa said, looking up.

Bog Girl went silent.

Helen put down her sewing needle, and coughed into the purple scarf the cards had been wrapped in, and Speck ran downstairs. He climbed onto Bog Girl's bed, raced along her headboard.

"Speck fell from a tree," Bog Girl continued.

"Yes," I said, "when he was a baby."

"You fed him from the smallest spoon," Bog Girl said.

Outside our windows, snow drifted over our rocks and vines; it erased the footprints I'd made coming and going from the forest; it was as cold and deep as death, and it changed the places we thought we knew, made them white.

Chapter Eight

The rainmaker, Mr. Benjamin McCoy, knocked on our door the next afternoon. He wore a flat cap and I noticed his face was red and worn as if it had been shaped by sun and wind. Mr. McCoy had spent his life repairing and selling things; he could arrange his features so they seemed at once friendly and honest. Our father said McCoy had made his way through four wives, all of whom left him, climbing onto horses or trains, their angry letters folded into envelopes they left on the kitchen table, their suitcases packed while he was at work. Our father said certain truths were absent from advertising.

"I make moisture," I heard McCoy tell my father, "but it may or may not fall as rain."

"I'll take what I can get," our father said.

Our father followed McCoy into the forest and I heard their voices out there, rising and falling, smelled our father's pipe burning as McCoy made his way up into the trees. Our snowman lingered on the lawn. He was a lopsided stack of circles with one long stick arm and one short one, facing east; snow drifted against our barn, and haunted the fields beyond, where our horses darkened. Our father had built a platform high in the canopy of a Clotho tree and Ben McCoy, an agile man, climbed the ladder of limbs. He and our father used ropes to deliver McCoy's secret ingredients. All day Frannie, Bog Girl, and I were aware of McCoy up there: dancing and singing, his pots of smoke filling the air with a smell that reminded me of old socks or cheese. This was the day before the Sunday when our father would host two funerals and drive the bodies of the old woman, who had fallen down a flight of stairs and into another world, and the middle-aged man, who ate a big dinner, but did not live to digest it, to the cemetery beyond Lost River where, he hoped, the Clotho coffins, and peat, and Ghost Pipe would combine with the dust in the church cellar, and two more of the dead would rise and return. If he could usher the dead back to the world of the living our father would be more powerful than a doctor, or priest, and Fergus told me one night, in the barn, where he leaned over his notes, his unlit pipe in his mouth, that he wanted to be a man who sold immortality instead of coffins. I could see this in the fine lines around his chocolate eyes when I found him before and after supper, among cats, bent over his frayed notebook, his pupils reflecting lantern light. I could see it when I found him wandering alone in the forest with his hands in his pockets: bent forward, listening to the wind.

"If only I could bring back the people we lost years ago," my father said to me once, on the porch, where we watched Speck nibbling a nut: his face in profile, one dark eye watchful. I knew he meant Great Aunt

Nora, who doted on Fergus all through his childhood, giving him boats, and chickens, and his enormous library of books, and, once, even his own hive of bees, which danced and kept his secrets. Nora came on long summer visits from West Virginia and Fergus waited for her ferry boat on our North Carolina island each June, watching the horizon like so many fishermen's wives.

At lunch our mother vanished to attend her first birth since Lucy's awakening: a teenage girl who would not reveal the father of her child, a girl who stayed in labor for two days, pacing and moaning in a cabin five miles from our own. Frannie and I cooked a lunch of ham, cornbread, cabbage, and boiled potatoes, but Bog Girl would only eat the potatoes; our father came in with his books and notes, shaking snow from his boots, and sat down beside her. Gossamer followed Bog Girl to the table and folded himself into the shadows beneath her chair.

"Should we take lunch to McCoy?" Frannie asked.

"Take him some of that cornbread," our father said.

"What are you reading?" I asked our father.

"*The Book of the Dead*," our father said.

"What's that?" Bog Girl asked.

"Egyptian spells to help the dead in the afterlife," our father said.

"Like when I was in the bog?" Bog Girl said.

"Yes," our father said. "The Egyptians thought the dead passed through gates and caverns guarded by crocodiles and monsters."

"Do you remember *being* dead?" Frannie asked Bog Girl.

"I remember running through the forest," Bog Girl said, "and tearing my dress."

"Were you being chased?" our father asked.

"I don't know," Bog Girl said.

"The God of the Dead in Egypt was named Osiris," our father said. "He was killed by his brother, Set, who wanted to steal his throne; Set cut Osiris into pieces and his wife, Isis, put him together again, revived him with a spell, and he returned to the living for a short time; I was trying to *find* the spell Isis used."

"Helen is in a completely white room," Bog Girl said.

"You can see her?" our father asked.

Bog Girl and Frannie and I carried lunch to Mr. McCoy in a pail. Bog Girl's cape billowed behind her in the wind and we all leaned forward as we crossed the lawn; Bog Girl stopped to adjust the stick arms on our snowman. She reshaped his tiny, lopsided head; the cold hurt her hands and yet she seemed most affectionate with snowmen and corpses.

"How is Helen?" I asked Bog Girl as we passed through the shadows at the edge of our forest.

"She liked the train ride through the mountains," Bog Girl said. "She had her own compartment and did some needlepoint. But she isn't sure about the sanatorium. She's supposed to spend most days resting in bed."

"So much white," Frannie said, her breath ghostly.

I thought of how Tuberculosis was sometimes called the White Death, about the white milk Bog Girl drank, and the white handkerchiefs I had seen Josie and Helen hold to their mouths. I thought of the white acres of heaven.

As we got closer to Mr. McCoy in his tree, we could hear singing and smell smoke. I could hear him playing harmonica up there: his mouth blowing, his hands cupping sound.

"Mr. McCoy?" I yelled.

Bog Girl held his lunch pail, and wore her cape, and she might have been Red Riding Hood at the edge of the forest, walking towards the wolf, carrying cake and wine; the trees around us were tall and hushed and they pierced the sky.

"Mr. McCoy?" I called.

"I'll take it to him," Bog Girl said, hoisting herself onto the lowest branch.

"Are you sure?" Frannie asked, wanting to make the climb herself. Trees beckoned to Frannie.

Bog Girl did not respond; we heard her feet, and the sound of branches creaking; we heard Mr. McCoy chanting.

Long ago, our father taught us the names for death in other places. Darkesville had the Grim Reaper in his black cape, carrying a scythe, but the Irish had Donn, who drowned in the sea, and lived in the Otherworld, causing storms. The Chinese had Meng Po who brewed a tea of amnesia to help a soul forget their previous life before embarking on another, and the Etruscans had Aito: a demon with the head of a wolf who led the dead to the Underworld. I thought of these creatures when there was a sound above our heads and snow fell and I saw Bog Girl lose her footing and tumble through the branches. Her falling was both fast and slow; it seemed as if Frannie and I might be able to stop it, but Bog Girl landed with a heavy thud before we could intervene. She fell through the spaces between branches; she seemed to fall through time. She was not like Gossamer and the other barn cats who righted themselves in the air: the triangles of their ears alert, their paws beneath them before they touched the earth. Bog Girl fell on her back with a cold thud, her arms open, her blue cape fanning over the snow. Frannie and I looked down at her; Frannie reached for Bog Girl's hand while Mr. McCoy descended carefully. I could see his work boots moving on the icy branches.

"Is she breathing?" Mr. McCoy asked.

Bog Girl's eyes were closed but her breath was nearly celestial as it bloomed.

Our father went to fetch Dr. Saunders while Mr. McCoy carried Bog Girl to her bed by the fire, where Gossamer had been waiting, and we wrapped her in blankets.

"Can you feel your arms and legs?" McCoy asked.

"Yes," Bog Girl said.

"Does anything hurt?" he asked.

Bog Girl shook her head.

"My brother fell from a tree when we were kids," McCoy told us. "He broke an arm, and a leg, and he hit his head so hard he didn't wake up for two days."

When Dr. Saunders arrived, in his winter trench coat, carrying his black bag and a half-eaten apple, the rest of us stepped outside so he could examine Bog Girl. Mr. McCoy smoked a cigarette on our porch, its ash growing long, and our father beckoned for Frannie and me to follow him into the barn; I walked in the path his boots made in the snow, and Frannie walked in my footprints, so we left the trail of a single person with strange, misshapen feet.

Our father asked us to weave Ghost Pipe into a crown for the dead old woman and the middle-aged man and Frannie and I stood together at his tall wooden work table, braiding; the old woman and the middle aged man had grown cold in their boxes of silence, and they went on, as the newly dead do, trying to disappear. Dr. Saunders opened the barn door and stood in the entryway. From our perch in the back workroom we heard our father greet him.

"She seems fine," Dr. Saunders said. "I'm not sure of how her body will deal with injuries. Right now there's no concussion or broken bones; call me if she gets headaches or has trouble with her balance."

"Anne says it was a long fall," our father said.

"At least she fell in the snow," Dr. Saunders said. He removed the half-eaten apple from his coat pocket and took a bite.

Chapter Nine

McCoy's light rain turned to ice on the day of the funerals; our mother had come home from delivering a baby boy, who was born with an umbilical cord wrapped around his neck like a noose; she said the cord, which she cut as fast as she could, had nearly strangled him. In my imagination the cord became a vine, and the vine grew leaves. I remembered the story of my own birth: how my life had nearly extinguished my mother's. Frannie was closer to Ariel than I was, more like her, and I wondered sometimes if this had been determined by the smoothness of her birth; I had nearly killed our mother while Frannie arrived swiftly and politely. Ariel's shoulders sagged and she was still wearing an apron splattered with blood; she was heating oatmeal on the stove.

"I was carrying lunch up to Mr. McCoy, and my feet slipped," Bog Girl said.

"It was good she fell in the snow," I said.

"You fell from the *top* of the tree?" our mother asked.

"Near the top," Bog Girl said.

"Oatmeal?" our mother asked.

"Milk, please," Bog Girl said. I noticed that she was polite with our mother.

Frannie and I prepared the parlor for the funerals, which would be performed one after the other; we placed hymns on the piano, flowers on the mantle, and apple pies on the stove; we covered the mirrors and stopped the clocks, while our mother and Bog Girl rested upstairs. When it was time to load the bodies in the wagon and visit the cemetery, Bog Girl asked to come along, and our parents could think of no reason why she shouldn't. We did not ride as close to Lost River as we usually do because a slick coating of ice had formed along the banks, but our father tried to retrace his path through the forest to the cemetery, hoping something restorative lingered in the air. At the cemetery Bog Girl stood under the tent with Frannie and me; mourners came to shake her hand.

"You're the one who rose from the dead?" a man without teeth asked.

Bog Girl nodded.

"What was it like," he asked her, "on the other side?"

"I was never hungry," Bog Girl said.

After the minister spoke, and the mourners sang *Abide With Me*, the bodies of the deceased were carried down to the same cold cellar where Bog Girl and Lucy once awaited their burials. The gravediggers shut the door, and the minister began to pray fervently, while his wife mopped his brow with a handkerchief. Then, we went home to await news: through the forest, past our dissolving snowman, whose stick arms now pointed at the ground; our horses pulled hard against the coming darkness, which was closing over our house, and inside we found Josie and Louisa sitting in front of our living room fireplace.

"I hope you don't mind," Louisa said to our mother, "we were passing by."

We were removing our mittens when Beatrice Mallicoat appeared at our door in a wide brimmed hat with Lucy in her arms. "Lucy took a bad fall yesterday," we heard her say to our mother.

"Really?" our mother said. I could see her thinking about Bog Girl's hard descent into snow.

"She climbed into our loft when I was checking something in the oven and fell from the top of the ladder," Mrs. Mallicoat said.

"When they're little it seems like you can't turn your back for a minute," Louisa said.

"How's Helen?" Beatrice asked Louisa.

Lucy ran to Bog Girl, buried her face in her cape, and they sat together at the kitchen table, speaking with their hands beside a lantern our mother lit, their fingers casting shadows on the wall. Though they lived among us, it was easy to see that Bog Girl and Lucy were more related to one another. Sometimes I found them speaking to each other in this sign language known only to themselves. In spring, when Frannie and I took them into the forest to perform fairy tales, they disappeared into the canopy and we could hear them speaking to people we could not see. Once, on a hike, they disappeared through brambles and thicket to an underground cave and did not return for hours. Frannie and I called and called for them, our voices like wind in the leaves. Lucy and Bog Girl had both fallen, as if their fates were dizzy, off balance: one from a ladder in the house, the other from a ladder of branches; they had fallen, but they appeared unharmed.

"Could we play *Button, Button*?" Josie asked me.

"Go up to your room," my mother said. "We'll bring you tea."

"Bog Girl doesn't like tea," Josie said.

"She might drink hot chocolate," Frannie said.

"*You're* the one who likes hot chocolate," I said.

Upstairs, I found Speck asleep on our bed, in his nest of socks; we woke him when we came into the room, and shut the window, and he began to climb the furniture, then Josie's shoulders, pausing for a moment on top of her head.

"Speck thinks I'm Helen," Josie said. "Animals like her best."

I opened a wooden box on the bureau and found our button.

"We're supposed to sit in a circle," I said.

Lucy went to the dollhouse and rearranged the bedroom, placing the tiny bed in a corner beside the piano; Bog Girl lingered beside our bookshelf, pulling down books.

"What's this one about?" she asked.

"That's *Alice in Wonderland*," I said. "It's about a girl who falls down a rabbit hole into another world."

I thought of Alice falling, as Bog Girl had, a rabbit's hole becoming a tunnel to another world. Bog Girl turned the pages of the book, pausing to examine the pictures of the White Rabbit running, with his pocket watch, and the Mad Hatter in his top hat presiding over a tea party.

"What's this?" Bog Girl asked, pulling a second book off the shelf.

"That's *The Wizard of Oz,*" I said.

"We got it for Christmas last year," Frannie said, "and Papa read it to us that night. It's about a girl taken away by a tornado who lands in a city called Oz."

"Can you read?" I asked Bog Girl, who was turning the pages with interest.

"I don't know," Bog Girl said. "Maybe I used to?"

"I could teach you," Frannie said.

"Where's the button?" Josie said; she was impatient.

"Button," Lucy said.

"Sit beside me, Lucy," Frannie said.

"Button, button, who has the button?" Josie said.

Then, she walked behind us, pretending to give the button to each of us, and we pretended to receive it, though only one person had it hidden in her fist; we took turns guessing who that person might be. I could always tell by looking at Frannie's flushed face whether or not she held the button, but Frannie could not read me so easily. I found, as I grew older, I could keep a secret, even from myself.

I left the game to go to the bathroom, wandered downstairs to see if our hot chocolate was warming in a pot on the stove. I carried a lantern and I could see the shadow of myself descending; I imagined my shadow was my doppelgänger, who was a darker, weightless version of me, sliding along walls and floorboards. My father told me Queen Elizabeth saw her own doppelgänger, laid out on her bed, in her great golden gown, a few days before she died. I could hear the adults speaking in hushed voices.

"Lucy sees things that are going to happen *before* they happen," Beatrice said.

"Like what?" Louisa asked.

"She told me to be careful with my left hand today," Beatrice said, "and then I burned it, while I was ironing."

"Bog Girl seems to know what's happening to Helen," my mother said.

"It's a bit odd that Bog Girl fell from the top of a tree," our father said, "and then Lucy fell from a ladder."

"What if Bog Girl and Lucy help me with my fortune telling this spring?" Louisa said.

Each spring, Louisa sat in a caravan, at the edge of a carnival, among other Irish families, reading Tarot cards.

"I keep trying to figure out what was *different* about the burial of Lucy and Bog Girl," our father said.

"What if you could save everyone in our village?" Beatrice said.

"I don't know if all the dead *should* be saved," our mother said. "How would there be room for the living?"

For weeks after this I dreamed of the dead returning to earth in such numbers that there were not enough beds or dresses or chairs. I dreamed of the dead eating dinner before the living and leaving only scraps behind: crumbs from a cake, bones of a pork chop, the pale, shattered fragments of an eggshell.

Chapter Ten

In the mild light of dawn I heard the sound of our father stirring the fires in our house before leaving for the cemetery. Somewhere, downstairs, Bog Girl already knew whether or not the dead had returned to us, but she slept heavily, her face pressed against the soft forgetfulness of her pillow. I heard our mother stirring a pot of something. I heard Speck scratching at the window, his arboreal life calling.

It would be an hour before we discovered that the old woman and the middle- aged man had risen during their long night, but their awakening was short lived; they stood up just long enough to open the doors of their coffins, and stand in the haze of that deep, cold room, but they had fallen again, before dawn, into their eternal slumber, and though Dr. Saunders was called in to examine them, he could find no signs of life: the old woman was still dead of her broken neck, and the middle-aged man was still infected by the explosion in his gallbladder. The newspapers, later, would report these resurrections as a hoax, the journalists suggesting that someone came in the darkness to disturb the bodies; the villagers of Darkesville were also certain the bodies had not moved of their own accord, but had been tampered with by the living. Only we Van Beests felt sure that, for a moment, they had lived.

The minister, George, and his wife, Edna, stood at the top of the cellar staircase expectantly, without the wine cask, dressed in anticipation. The minister had, I'm sure, imagined the expansion of his congregation, and his own widening fame, the way our father imagined his ability to bring all of us back from sickness and accidents like a God; our father had read to us the story of Jesus finding Lazarus four days dead, behind a stone, after a long illness. He told us how Jesus brought Lazarus back to the world of taxes and feasts, just as Snow White rose up from her glass coffin when she was kissed by a prince: the poison apple dislodged from her throat, her body remembering sunlight and wind. The living are concerned with objects and status, but the dead eat pomegranates and forget. Bog Girl liked stories as much as I did because, she said, they had a beginning, middle, and end. She liked moonlight and shadows; she liked winter, when everything was dormant and hidden, even though the cold caused her to shiver. Having returned to the living after a hibernation in the peat Bog Girl would never be a woman, yet she would wander among mortals for generations; I wondered how it felt to be timeless: locked forever in girlhood, without a clear birth or old age.

"It *almost* worked," I heard our father say to our mother at breakfast, "but I was missing something."

"Maybe it only works for *children*," our mother said, "or people who die in a particular way."

"They woke up," our father said, "I was *so* close."

Fergus went out to his barn, where he spent many weeks after this, making notes at his desk, nibbling chocolate, and reading; the old woman and the middle-aged man appeared to him in dreams: washing their clothes in Lost River, building furniture out of snow.

"What was the temperature on the day Lucy and Bog Girl were supposed to be buried?" our father asked me one afternoon.

"It wasn't too cold," I said, "maybe forty or fifty?"

"The newspaper would know," he said, standing up, and walking away, leaving the barn door ajar. One of the spotted cats followed, pausing briefly to rub her whiskers against a coffin.

Our first letter arrived from Helen, written on folded, peach stationary with sketches of birds in the margins. Helen began sending a weekly missive from the sanatorium, and Frannie and I anticipated the journey up the narrow lane to our mailbox. I liked the delicate rustle of paper being pulled from an envelope, the Vulcan ink from Helen's fountain pen, the way the letter had been touched by her soft hands.

Bog Girl walked with Frannie and me when we went to check for letters, though sometimes, headed back towards the house, she wandered into the forest and remained there for an hour or more; when she returned, Gossamer or Speck at her heels, her braids were undone and her face was flushed.

"What do you *do* in the forest?" Frannie asked. She was working on a needlepoint picture of a rose.

"I remember things," Bog Girl said.

"What things?" I asked.

Bog Girl shrugged.

I read the letters from Helen aloud at the table, where Bog Girl ate potatoes, or pickled eggplant, while the rest of us devoured ham with brussels sprouts, or ham with cabbage; we drank tea while she drank her milk with honey.

"Dear Van Beests," I read, "I'm still trying to get used to the routines here; the nurses are strict and they make us spend the whole day resting, eating, and breathing fresh air. I have never eaten so much in my life: cheeses, meats, chocolates, ice cream, glasses of milk with every meal. I think I'm getting fat. My corsets are tight. We drink milk every afternoon on the veranda in lounge chairs, wrapped in blankets, sunning ourselves, even if it's snowing. I don't understand why it's healthy to sunbathe in winter. People are dying of their coughs, though we're not supposed to speak of death, since this might ruin morale. They took us horseback riding yesterday, in a forest where the trees are always green, and I have knitted a scarf for Speck though I know he will not wear it. I am drawing pictures of all the hats I see here for Josie and I have made friends with an older man named Oliver who used to work as a navigator on a ship that went to Africa. We have been trading books during rest time, which goes on all afternoon. They showed us a moving picture one night, called *The Count of Monte Cristo*, which was one of the oddest things I've ever seen. There was music, and the story was about a sailor, and I think Anne would have loved it. One of the doctors here has a watch attached to his wrist and he lets me touch it whenever he is listening to my lungs. I hope all is well in Darkesville. What do Lucy and Bog Girl think of winter? Have you been playing Hide and Seek? How is Speck? These, and other things, I wonder. Love, Helen."

"It's good she's eating," our mother said. "She was so thin."

I looked at Bog Girl's glass of milk and thought of Helen drinking milk: white in her cup, white in her lungs.

Our father began teaching Bog Girl to read. He sat in his deep leather chair in the evenings, beside our bed, his lantern flickering, his pipe in his mouth, and as he read stories aloud, he passed them to Bog Girl, who sat beside him in a small chair he had fashioned for her in the barn. He read a sentence, then she repeated the sentence, her finger moving under the words. I liked to imagine I was Bog Girl, warming myself under our father's gaze.

"Once upon a time there was a poor widow who lived in a cottage with her only son, Jack," our father read. Then, he passed the book to Bog Girl who ran her finger over the text, repeating. Many nights Frannie and I fell asleep like this: our stories told in two voices, the beanstalk growing twice outside Jack's window, where a kingdom of giants swayed above. Bog Girl seemed to like *Jack and the Beanstalk*, so we heard it a half dozen times: how Jack traded his family cow for a handful of magic beans, how his mother threw the beans into the yard, and called her son a fool, and how, overnight, the beans sprouted: a great stalk growing so tall it pierced the heavens, its branches bearing a kingdom of wealthy giants.

It was around this time, as Bog Girl was remembering how to read, her voice growing more confident when she ran her finger under the text, that she began to have trouble sleeping. When our mother was awakened by a father rapping on our front door, in the middle of the night, fetching her for a birth, she found Bog Girl upright beside the fire, watching the embers dwindle. Our father found her, at dawn, in the barn, where she was trying out each of the coffins, as Goldilocks had tried out the beds in the house of the three bears. Bog Girl mixed up her days and nights, which our mother said was something babies were prone to, after emerging from the steady darkness of the womb. We found Bog Girl napping in the morning, but awake in the winter night, which pressed frostily against our windows and doors; she was like the dancing princesses, who opened their floor at night instead of sleeping, and descended to a kingdom of music; she said she heard something in the forest that made it hard for her to be still.

It was February when the flu came to Darkesville, by train, on the coat of a man from a nearby village. He had come to stay with his brother, and though he had only a sniffle and a scratchy throat, his nieces and nephews came down with high fevers and coughs, and their mother and Auntie, who held them through the night, found themselves suspended in their own high fevers, and buried themselves under blankets, while the blizzards of winter continued: our horses confined to their stables, our porch glittering in the moonlight. The flu was passed on the heads of dogs, and in envelopes, and on newspapers, and on the saddles of horses, and it moved with increasing frequency as the days grew longer: by Model T, on fruit, on bottles of milk and boxes of cookies. In our house, on Orchard Ridge Road, we could not see it coming, or hear it over the protests of the wind, though the news of the first cases reached us through

Jasper's radio, in the Scarborough living room, where we heard descriptions of hospitals without enough beds, and victims who took ill at dinnertime, and did not live to see morning.

Soon, the days would grow longer: light spilling through our windows, falling across the quilt of the bed I shared with Frannie, and we would both grow taller, our dresses too short, though Bog Girl would stay the same size, and Lucy, on her plump legs, would grow wiser, but would go on looking like a baby who walked too soon: her hair in irritated tufts that refused to lengthen, two teeth appearing in her mouth so, when she ate, she reminded me of Speck, nibbling a nut. In spring wild animals would step out of our forest, awakened by hunger, and corpses would arrive in our barn with increasing frequency, and the apple orchards, to the west, would grow gravid with blossoms. But during these last weeks of winter Bog Girl read *The Jungle Book*, pausing over the descriptions of panthers and bears, and felt her body refusing to sleep. One night, when I walked downstairs with my candle to fetch a glass of water, I found her reading without a light, and asked how she could see the words.

"I see without my eyes," Bog Girl said, and I did not ask what she meant by this, but climbed the stairs to my room, where Frannie was already breathing like the sea.

Chapter Eleven

It was harder for Lucy to reach us in the depths of winter, so Bog Girl seemed relieved when there was a thaw in March and Lucy appeared again, dressed in mittens and stockings, her unruly hair tamed. They were glad to see one another, and Bog Girl took Lucy for a walk in the forest, which was turning the newest shade of green. Beatrice remained with our mother and I noticed she had small watery eyes and an upturned nose that had grown pink at the tip.

"Lucy hasn't been sleeping well," I heard Beatrice say to our mother. "How was the birth?"

"The delivery was easy, but the babies were small," our mother said. "Two girls."

"Twins," Beatrice said, shaking her head. "Who's the mother?"

"Mary Basnight," my mother said. "She thought she was just having one; the second was a *surprise*."

"I find Lucy awake in the middle of the night," Beatrice said, "just wandering."

"Bog Girl has been sleepless too," our mother said, "I wonder why?"

"It worries me," Beatrice said. "The neighbors think Lucy is so odd. I mean, she looks like an infant but she can walk and talk. She's a baby but not a baby; she can't seem to grow."

When the snow receded, wild animals stepped out of the forest. One morning, Frannie and I went out to feed the horses their oats and we passed a flock of turkeys with bald heads and stick legs; one walked faster than the others, his blue chin wagging. At twilight a fox with an elegant red tail slipped out of the foliage, blinked his liquid eyes, and disappeared. I had been sitting in my bedroom window, reading, and I looked up just in time to see him vanish, his tail like the hem of a royal robe. On this day, while Frannie and I jumped rope on the porch, and Speck darted through the yard, a mother bear emerged: an enormous shadowy creature who seemed to have formed herself from winter's darkness, her two cubs lumbering behind her on carpeted legs; Frannie and I stood still, as we'd been taught, watching them pass; they must have come from the caves to the west, beyond the orchards. The mother looked as if she'd been asleep for years and now the world and its colors surprised her. It occurred to me that each spring was a resurrection, that the hibernating animals were like Bog Girl and Lucy, rising from a sleep as deep as death. Frannie and I waited until the mother bear turned towards the forest, her cubs shifting behind her the way starlings shift together in the sky. Then, we ran into the house where our mother and Beatrice were chopping potatoes and collards. Beatrice looked wide beside our mother who was eternally thin and elegant, her cornflower dress pressed and neat.

"You have a bit of dirt on your face," she said to me, spitting on her finger and reaching for my cheek.

"A bear and her cubs," I said, "just passed by our house; they went into the forest."

"She was huge," Frannie said. "Her babies were the size of *hippos*."

"Lucy," Beatrice said, putting down her knife. Her brown, curly hair had come free from its tight bun.

Our mother walked to the window and looked out at the lawn, which was empty now, without any trace of those powerful animals. If Frannie had not been with me I might have disbelieved my own memory of them.

"Go tell your father, Anne," my mother said.

I ran, as messengers do. Throughout my life, messages would arrive for me: by letter, or telegram. Some were preceded by a ringing telephone or a knock on the door. Our father told us that messengers were sometimes killed if they brought bad news; he told us about Hermes, in Greek Mythology, delivering messages in winged shoes; I flung open the barn door.

My father took his shotgun down from the nails above the door and walked into the forest; I watched his back disappear between two white Clotho trees. While he was gone, a wagon pulled up in front of the barn and I could see a body wrapped in quilts. Our mother left Beatrice chopping collards in the kitchen and went out to meet the driver: a man our father's age, in a wide-brimmed hat and trench coat. I saw Ariel open the doors to the barn and nod to the man who carried a wrapped body into the room full of hay, and cats, and coffins. I saw the man stand there a long time, not wanting to leave. Our mother closed the door and left him there; when she returned, she washed her hands and face for a long time, water dripping from her chin into the kitchen sink.

"That's the postman, Mr. Winters. His wife was just my age and she just died of the flu," our mother said.

Frannie and I stood at the window, watching for signs of our father or Bog Girl or Lucy. We wondered if the bears might return to our acres on their way home to distant caves and orchards.

"I don't know how Fergus is going to prepare the body without catching this stuff," our mother said.

"He could refuse," Beatrice said.

"He won't," our mother said.

I could see a boy in a brown uniform walking towards our house, with a package in his arms.

"Someone is coming," Frannie said, her nose pressed to glass, her breath a cobweb.

"The day doesn't lack excitement," our mother said, drying her hands on her apron.

We went to the porch, and the boy with the package grew larger, until he stood before us.

"Are you sure you have the right address?" our mother asked.

"I'm delivering your telephone," the boy said.

"Oh," our mother said, "I forgot."

"We're getting a telephone?" I asked.

"Your father ordered one," our mother said.

"Would you like a bowl of collards?" Beatrice asked the delivery boy. "A glass of tea?"

"Tea please," the delivery boy said.

"A telephone!" Frannie said.

"Are they hard to install?" our mother asked.

"We just saw a bear," I said to the delivery boy.

"Your father wanted a Model T but I told him I'd rather have a phone," our mother said.

Then, I remembered those first days after Lucy and Bog Girl returned to us, when my parents began to dream of the things they might own if our father's business was successful: the cars, and jewelry, fine china and copper pots, silk dresses and suits. Our mother had bought herself a new shirtwaist and trench coat; she bought little pots of rouge for her cheeks and a box of cigars for our father. The living are confined to a world of objects, and must return, continuously, to their dinner tables; but the dead, who lived in our forest, needed no houses or gardens; they did not need firelight, or candles, or lanterns, and they did not need to be careful because, like Bog Girl, they could see without their eyes.

I followed the telephone delivery boy, and asked questions about how telephones worked, until, exasperated, he pulled a bag of marbles from his pocket and showed Frannie and me how to place them on a circular rug in the parlor where we took turns trying to knock them off by flicking one marble at another; I liked holding the marbles up to the light where they glittered like eyes.

Once the telephone was installed, Frannie and I found we could stand in a corner of the kitchen while the stews were simmering, or the pies were baking, and listen to people talking to each other all over Darkesville. We heard a woman named Cora describe a case of the gout in her big toe to Dr. Saunders. We heard Janet Eastman tell William Smith that she *would* allow him to take her for a drive on Sunday. We heard a military officer inform a mother that her son had died of a fever in the Great War and was being sent home by train. Frannie and I liked listening to the conversations of villagers, liked this escape from our own lives. It was the same kind of escape we found in the stories our father read to us at night. It was the sort of escape we experienced, a few years later, when we heard stories and music seeping through a radio, the voices disembodied, like the voices of ghosts. We went on cooking supper after the telephone boy put on his jacket in the entryway, and after Mr. Winters closed the barn door and rode back to his empty house, where the fires had gone out, and the bed was cold and nothing simmered on the stove. Mr. Winters was the postman and he would return to his life of sealed white envelopes, sorted into boxes with golden doors, and carts full of packages, tied with twine, waiting to be delivered. Frannie and I set the table and stood at the window, watching.

"I was foolish to send Lucy for a walk," Beatrice said; she had brought her knitting with her, and her wide back was beside our mother's narrow one as she and Ariel shared a bench in front of our fireplace, their needles clicking; Frannie liked knitting, and sometimes took out her own needles, and sat beside our mother: her precision inherited along with her long, accurate fingers. But, this night, Frannie kept vigil by the window instead, watching the shadows on the lawn lengthen. The first creature to emerge from the woods was Gossamer, who walked on soft paws towards our porch, and he was followed by Bog Girl and Lucy, who chased one another, Bog Girl's cape floating behind her, her braids unfastened. Frannie and I went onto the porch to meet them.

"Where's Dad?" Frannie asked.

"We didn't see him," Bog Girl said.

"He was looking for you," I said. "There were bears."

"We saw a mother and her cubs when we were jumping rope," Frannie said. "The mother was huge."

"We met them," Bog Girl said, "I helped them find blackberries."

Beatrice and our mother had come to the door, their half-knitted scarves and socks abandoned, their needles still.

"You're not supposed to *play* with bears," Beatrice said. "A mother bear will kill to protect her cubs."

"The mother bear was *hungry,*" Lucy explained.

Our father emerged from the forest: his rifle over his shoulder, a dead blackbird under one arm.

"There you are," he said to Bog Girl.

"Did you see the bears?" I asked.

"I shot a blackbird," our father said, "but I didn't see the bears."

When he came to the porch, Bog Girl and Lucy reached out their hands to touch the dead bird's feathers, which were lifted by the evening wind.

"Can I hold it?" Lucy asked.

"Lucy and Bog Girl helped the bears find blackberries," our mother said.

"Bears look cute," our father said, "but you can't play with them; wild animals are unpredictable; you must keep a respectful distance."

Lucy and Bog Girl nodded, but something in their eyes glittered with defiance, and reminded me of the eyes of the bears as they had crossed our lawn, their noses pointed towards tangled, untamed places.

Chapter Twelve

Frannie and I woke to the sound of our parents arguing, in their bedroom down the hall.

"You'll place the whole family in danger," our mother said.

"I'm a mortician," our father said, "I work with the *deceased*."

"This flu is bad," our mother said.

"You'll have me turn away bodies?" our father said. "People die of it every year."

"Not like this," our mother said. "You won't earn a living if you're dead."

Our mother's voice was sharp and high; in arguments she often prevailed over our father who was milder and less passionate. It was strange to hear our parents raise their voices because they were usually amorous and intwined. Frannie and I often found the two of them holding hands in the yard, beneath a Copper Beech tree. He liked to kiss the nape of her neck when she was doing dishes, or run his finger over the underside of her wrist at the dinner table. I saw them dancing together sometimes, in front of the fireplace, when they thought Frannie and I had gone to bed, their shadows growing long against the wall. Some women had begun wearing long-waisted or free-flowing dresses but our mother, who was naturally slender and a bit vain, had ordered a Coraline Health Corset which she said allowed her to be vigorous but keep her figure. Our father quite clearly admired this figure and liked to watch her baking: each ingredient measured carefully then poured or sifted into a wooden bowl. She liked watching him light a pipe in one neat gesture or roll up a newspaper and swat a fly.

That day, instead of disappearing into the barn alone to tend Mr. Winters' wife, our father took Bog Girl with him. Our parents agreed that Bog Girl was not like the rest of us; she had fallen from the top of a tree and still she lived. She did not catch our sore throats or coughs. As the flu victims arrived, our father taught Bog Girl how to prepare the bodies for viewing and burial; he instructed her, standing among the skinny cats, told her exactly how much of each preservative to mix together, and they rode together through the forest, to the bog, where Bog Girl stood over the mystery of her own origins, with a shovel. At night, in our armchair, they practiced reading together, about how Mowgli did not know the ways of man because he had been raised in the jungle. When she could not sleep, Bog Girl slipped into the back rooms of our barn, in darkness, to tend Mrs. Winters, and then so many others, who caught the flu at a church social, or the country store, caught it at a garden party, or from the keys of a piano, caught it at the store where they stopped to buy flour or a sack of sugar.

Our mother invited the Scarboroughs to dinner and they arrived in the evening, just Josie and Louisa, without Jasper, who was a member of the volunteer fire department and had been called away, by the ringing of bells, to a grease fire in a kitchen at the other end of Darkesville. We were frightened of the flu and our mother made Bog Girl wash her face and hands for a long time in the sink; she gave her a huge overcoat that Bog Girl wore instead of her cape when she worked on bodies and, before she came in the house, she hung the overcoat limply on a hook on the barn wall.

Frannie and I were forbidden to enter the barn, even to deliver messages. In town, Mr. Winters, stricken with fear and grief, began suggesting that all mail to Darkesville be held; he told the people who came to collect packages or buy stamps that they might be buying a ticket to the next world. In my mind, all envelopes became tickets, waiting to be torn.

"The newspaper says they're thinking about discontinuing the mail," Louisa said, cutting into our mother's roast, which rose like an island out of a brackish gravy of potatoes and carrots; our father's crisp blackbird rested on its own platter.

"The roast is tough," our mother said, her fork disappointed.

"It's nice, Ariel," our father said.

"How will we get letters from Helen?" I asked.

"If I could just remember exactly how I prepared Bog Girl and Lucy I could *save* some of these people," our father said.

"You don't know that," our mother said. "It might have been possible only *once*."

"Imagine if the dead had their own country," Bog Girl said.

I tried to imagine this: the dead and wild animals gathered together in the wordless liminal spaces where twilight gives way to darkness or a meadow gives way to a forest.

There was a hush, during which we could hear the wind become a wolf. We could hear our knives and forks scraping against our plates.

"Helen will be home next Thursday," Louisa said.

"Can we have a party?" Frannie asked.

"She must be doing so much better," our mother said.

"I don't know," our father said. "It's not a great idea to have gatherings."

"Are you sure the mashed potatoes aren't too milky?" my mother asked.

"Can we meet her train?" I asked.

I had always wanted to visit the train station where I imagined portmanteaus and handsome women in chiffon dresses with feathered hats. The telephone began to ring.

"I can't get used to that *ringing*," our mother said, rising to answer it, the hem of her dress swishing, while the rest of us went on cutting and chewing. Bog Girl sat at the end of the table consuming her bowl of potatoes and her wintery glass of honey and milk. During the last blizzard I had seen Bog Girl experimentally place snow in a cup and try to drink it; she had licked the ice then spit it out again, her black eyes full of confusion.

"Not everything white tastes like milk," I had said.

"There's a baby," our mother said, when she hung up.

"Whose?" our father asked.

"Elizabeth Aldridge," our mother said. "She got married last spring; they think the baby's early."

We watched our mother walk to the coat rack in the entryway, her long golden hair lit by firelight. She reached for her pea coat.

"The younger women are often wrong about how long they've been pregnant," our mother said, "sometimes they don't even know they're pregnant, for sure, until the quickening, and by then their math is faulty. There's an apple pie in the oven; I hope the crust isn't too thick. You should check it in a half hour."

Our mother opened the front door, and all the candle flames on the table leaned for a moment before it closed again: blown sideways, their undersides as white as a rabbit's tail.

Chapter Thirteen

Spring came to North Mountain and one day, after our father left Frannie and me to accomplish our reading and math, we abandoned our books and chalk and slates at the kitchen table and went into the parlor to practice a piano duet we had been learning from Josie instead. I liked practicing piano in the parlor, where a stern grandfather clock kept time, and the red carpet had gone pink near our windows, bleached by the sun. I liked the stiff, carved furniture in that room which had once belonged to Great Aunt Nora, who was widowed young by a mustached man, Jack, who worked for the railroad until he died of appendicitis. I opened the piano bench, searching for our music, and found a fragment of a letter Nora had written fifty years before in which she described a place by the banks of Lost River where she sometimes saw her dead husband drinking water from his cupped hands. She said he smiled at her, and waved, and she could feel a great love emanate from him before he disappeared between rocks, into a shelter cave. I showed the letter to Frannie, and we leaned

window she made a chittering sound, deep in her throat, and went to lie down beside it, her arms around its slender neck. Frannie and I had been hanging laundry on a clothesline nearby, our white sheets breathing in the wind. We worried that the mother deer would reject her baby when she found it smelling like Bog Girl, and we worried that the doe would come home to find Bog Girl with her arms wrapped around her speckled fawn; the high grasses rippled like an ocean and I unfolded the sheets, then handed them to Frannie, who pinned them to the line. Our mother was away, delivering a baby, and our father had gone to visit with the minister and his wife at the rectory. Frannie and I beheld Bog Girl, who appeared happy in the deep eddies of the moving grasses, with her arms around a wild animal, and we watched the fawn, as it nuzzled with Bog Girl, just as it might with its own mother: its nose against her neck, its eyes closed. There seemed to be some understanding between beasts and the recently dead, as if they shared a common ancestor with fur, or hooves, or whiskers, in the valley from which the living are excluded. When the mother doe returned she was undisturbed by Bog Girl and this is when Frannie and I guessed that Bog Girl's time in the bog might have given her the scent of the forest, or some other scent familiar to wild creatures; we saw that Bog Girl's presence pleased the deer. And when she returned from the meadow, with prairie grasses in the hood of her blue cape, Bog Girl was able to sleep for an hour, on her bed beside the fireplace. I also noticed that the more she worked with our father in the barn, the less she slept. We found her reading in a rocking chair, night or day. But when Bog Girl walked among the feral creatures, in the forest or meadow, sleep returned to her, as if she had been instructed by the forest and its beasts. Bog Girl looked happiest when Frannie and I found her with a creature, and the animals seemed to know her and seek her out, wherever she was. Even Speck left our bed at night to locate Bog Girl; even he preferred her slender shoulder to my own.

"I don't know if we should tell Mom and Dad that she touched a fawn," I said to Frannie.

"If she does it in front of them, she'll get in trouble," Frannie said.

The day Helen's train brought her home from the sanatorium, we went to see her. I had not ridden on a train but liked to see one whenever I could. I liked the stories of the bedroom Mary Todd Lincoln travelled in to attend President Lincoln's funeral, and the descriptions of dining cars with starched tablecloths. I liked the way time in each of our towns had to be synchronized because of their comings and goings. Still, no matter how I pleaded, our parents thought the train station itself was too dangerous with *all those travellers from faraway places* so we hiked through the forest to the Scarborough house: Fergus and Ariel ahead of us, his head taller than hers, her arm wrapped around his, the brim of his hat casting a shadow over his face, her skirts rustling in the weeds, while Frannie and Bog Girl and I followed; Bog Girl wanted to know how Frannie and I got our names.

"Mine means *from France* or *free one*," Frannie said. "Mom and Dad said I had a great-grandmother who grew up in Paris."

"I was named after two women from history: Anne Hutchinson, who was banished from the Massachusetts Bay Colony, and Anne Boleyn, who was the second wife of Henry the VIII," I said.

"Anne Boleyn was beheaded," Frannie said.

"Why did your parents name you after two unlucky women?" Bog Girl asked.

"They said they were *strong* women," I said.

"I want a name," Bog Girl said.

"You could name yourself," I said.

"You must have had a name," Frannie said, "before."

"It's not much use to me now," Bog Girl said, "since I can't remember it."

She furrowed her brow and narrowed her eyes and, for a moment, I could see how much Bog Girl lost when she sank down, breathless, into that peat; she'd lost her family, her origins. Rising up a second time she was someone else, someone stuck in a permanent late childhood with only a cape and her dark hair left to suggest who she might be; she could not grow up, or marry, or have children like Frannie and me and she did not seem to want these things. When I saw her touching the hair of the dead in our barn, or wrapping her arms around the wild beasts, I knew she yearned for things I could not understand.

Helen was standing in the doorway of the Scarborough house and her face was rounder, her hair redder. Josie joined her to wave at us, wearing a new hat decorated with flowers, and I noted that Josie had grown paler and more vague while Helen was away. Josie had picked at her dinner plate, rearranging her peas, while Helen was drinking glass after glass of milk on a veranda dappled with snow. We saw our parents shake hands with Helen, but when we reached the threshold Frannie and I screamed and hopped around. Even Bog Girl hugged Helen and Josie and she did not generally approve of hugging, as if her time in the bog had made human warmth dubious.

The Scarboroughs had a red tablecloth on their long dining room table and they lit a candelabra at the center. Louisa and Jasper ferried serving platters heaped with roasted chicken, green beans, mashed potatoes. Each plate was so shiny I could see our hunger reflected there. Our silverware glittered on folded white napkins. The adults had slender wine glasses and Jasper, who wore a jacket, uncorked a bottle.

"The mashed potatoes are for *you*," Louisa told Bog Girl. Louisa wore one of her best dresses which was pale blue with a plunging neckline. I saw our mother notice Louisa's clothes, which had been shipped from New York or Boston.

"You'll like them," I said, sitting down beside her, "they're a mix of potatoes and milk."

"How was the train ride?" Frannie asked Helen.

"There was a dining car," Helen said, "where I drank tea while riding backwards."

"We saw bears," I said.

"So did we," Josie said, "a mother and her cubs; I think it was their first spring outing."

"I showed them where the blackberries are growing," Bog Girl said.

"Bears are not pets," Jasper reminded Bog Girl.

"We told her," our father said.

"Will you miss the sanatorium?" I asked Helen.

"We had this schedule, so every day was more or less the same," Helen said. "It's good to be home."

I heard the sound of Bog Girl scraping the bottom of her bowl with her spoon.

"Bog Girl has been helping me with my business," our father said, "she has learned to read."

Frannie and I looked at one another, across the candlelit table, both of us wishing our father's stories were about us. Bog Girl was supposed to be temporary, not a real sibling, yet she had diverted our father's attention.

"We have a telephone," Frannie said.

"Have you ever listened to the conversations of our neighbors?" I asked.

"It's impolite to listen," our mother said.

"But so interesting," Louisa said, rising to take the dessert out of her oven.

Dessert was blackberry cobbler and only Bog Girl did not eat a dish of it, preferring another dollop of mashed potatoes. In each spoonful I could taste the forest in springtime, and the bears at the edge of our lawn, having stepped out of winter's white.

"This weekend is our first carnival," Louisa said. "I would be grateful if Bog Girl and Lucy could join me, in my fortune telling tent."

"I don't want to," Bog Girl said.

"You could help people by telling them a little of what you know," Louisa said. "You could just reveal the happy things."

"Bog Girl sees the future?" Helen asked.

"Maybe, but I can't remember the past," Bog Girl said.

"The future is more valuable," Louisa said.

"All the girls could go to the carnival," our mother said.

"It's outside," Louisa said, "in the open air."

"Bog Girl, do you know how old I will live to be and who I will marry?" Josie asked.

Bog Girl did not lift her head, but continued eating mashed potatoes: one soft, pale spoonful after another.

In the days before the carnival, Lucy came to visit Bog Girl several times. The bodies of flu victims had nearly vanished from our father's barn, so we believed the flu had blown away in the warmer air, though we would see later that this was wrong: it grew more virulent as we left our houses, clung to our skirts when we were lured out by flowers and light. Our father was alone, smoking and eating chocolate and building coffins; he read and reread his notes on resurrection. More than once, I saw the minister, George, waddle out of the forest, checking his pocket watch, and disappear into our father's barn, because, like our father, he wanted to understand the conditions that allowed the dead to return. He came and went along the same path we took to deliver bodies to his cemetery: on a road worn away by animals, beside Lost River, which was rising now, its water loud and fast.

One night I rose for a glass of water and found that Speck was not buried in his pile of socks between Frannie and me; I descended into the kitchen where, after filling my water glass, I turned to find Speck and Gossamer curled up on either side of Bog Girl's sleeping head. I saw she had been reading a book in the rocking chair and it was still open to *The Pied Piper of Hamelin* with its pictures of a German town, overcome by rats, whose mayor hired a stranger in a cape to get rid of them. The stranger was a Piper, who played an eerie lute music that led all the rats to the river, where they drowned. After the rats were dead, though, the mayor refused to pay the Piper, who retaliated by playing a song on his lute that caused the children of Hamelin to rise from their beds and cribs, a song that caused children to abandon their games on the front lawn, and climb down from the trees in their yards. The Piper led those children, who danced behind him as the rats had, drawn by the beauty of his music, which was meant especially for them. He ushered them out of the lives they knew and into the river, which opened like a door between mountains. The children were carried under and away, their heads disappearing beneath the surface; they found themselves in some deep, unbreathable place, without their parents or blankets, a place where they forgot their own names. I looked at the book and I looked at Speck, who had always slept beside my head, his paws on my shoulder.

The next day, Lucy came to see Bog Girl and we all went into the forest together. I suggested that we enact the story of *The Pied Piper*.

"I want to be the Piper," Bog Girl said.

"I'm always the Piper," Frannie protested.

"I won't play if I can't be the Piper," Bog Girl said, "I have a cape."

"Why does *that* matter?" Lucy asked.

"The real Piper had a cape," I said.

The Clotho trees watched us, their colossal leaves shivering in the spring breeze. The day was sunny but cold.

"I'll be the mayor," I said, knowing no one else would want that role. Lucy agreed to be the children; Frannie was the rats.

"There are rats everywhere," I yelled as Frannie ran about, pretending to twitch her tail. "Rats in my bed! Rats in my food! We must hire someone to get rid of the rats!"

Bog Girl stepped into the clearing in her blue cape and she pretended to carry a lute. "I will save the town of Hamelin," she said. She made a melodic sound, deep in her throat, and we could hear the birds trilling above us, in the high canopy. Frannie followed Bog Girl through the forest, and I saw that Bog Girl was headed towards the sound of Lost River; soon, we were all pretending to be rats, and we danced behind her: Lucy on her stout baby legs, Frannie in her green spring dress with her golden hair hanging long, and me, with my dark hair in a ponytail and my best spring sweater. We saw that Bog Girl's music attracted real animals: Speck, and two of his squirrel friends who leapt down from the branches above, Gossamer who rose from a nap, a fox who stuck its slender face and tall ears out of a hole, a wolf with gray eyes, and two slender deer, who came from the bog, drawn by Bog Girl's throaty sound and rippling blue cape. The birds above us blackened the sky.

"We have to stop," I said, when I saw the animals following Bog Girl, and heard the rushing of the river, but no one seemed to hear me. There was only the sound of Bog Girl's throaty music, the beating of wings, and the rush of Lost River pulsing towards summer: its currents fast, its eddies deep.

"Frannie," I said, "we can't let her lead these animals into the river." Frannie was dancing behind Lucy, who looked like the illustrations of children in Hamelin: hands in the air, feet leaping.

"We're pretending," Frannie said, "Bog Girl won't drown anyone."

"How do you know?" I said; I felt myself pulled forward, even as I resisted; I felt the way I did when I swam in the river in late summer and the current carried me to a distant shore.

"If she's pretending," I said, "why have *real* animals come out of the woods?"

"Animals like her," Frannie said, slightly out of breath.

"Bog Girl, stop," I said, but she continued: her cape flapping, her music rising from someplace deep.

"Piper, stop," I said, and I saw her pause, then turn.

"My name," Bog Girl said.

"Piper, don't drown the animals," I said.

"I would not drown animals," Bog Girl said, and she resumed her dancing, and her music, but she turned away from Lost River, and led us instead to the bog, her singing intoxicating. At the edge of the bog the animals sipped water, and studied their own reflections.

That night, the minister and his round-faced wife came to supper; they sat at one end of our table, with their napkins tucked under their double chins, and our mother served a bass our father caught in Lost River, with corn on the cob, and peaches, and potatoes; she filled our glasses with lemonade. Bog Girl drank a pale glass of milk.

"The volunteer fire department discovered a family that got trapped in the mountain pass during the last storm," the minister said. "Edna and I are letting them stay at the church until they're well enough to travel."

"They've had a hard time," Edna said. "They nearly starved during the blizzards, just like the Donner Party."

Lucy and Bog Girl sat together at the opposite end of the table with Moonflowers and Ghost Pipe in their hair. They ate potatoes and signed to one another, jabbing the air with their fingers.

"What's the Donner Party?" Frannie asked.

"They were a group of travellers who believed they were taking a shortcut to California," our father said, "but they got trapped by snowfall in the Sierra Nevadas."

"Did they starve?" I asked.

"Half survived," our father said, "but they had to resort to cannibalism."

"They *ate* each other?" Frannie asked.

Edna was nibbling her corn on the cob and her round face moved from one end of the cob to the other, little bits gathering between her teeth. Her husband had a single piece of corn stuck in his beard, just below his lip.

"Did I boil the corn too long?" our mother asked.

"Oh no," the minister said, dabbing at his beard with a napkin.

"I have written down the steps I took to preserve Bog Girl and Lucy," our father said, pulling out a folded piece of paper from his pocket. "If you can think of anything I left out, I'd be grateful."

The minister held the list up to the light, pulled his glasses from his pocket.

"You girls seem to be doing well," Edna said to Lucy and Bog Girl.

"We played in the forest today," Bog Girl said. When she spoke, Gossamer rose from the bed by the fireplace and came to rub his face against her skirts.

"I did say a special prayer over the girls," the minster said.

"You blessed us," Bog Girl said, "with water from the Lost River."

"How do you know that?" the minister asked.

"It's one of my first memories," Bog Girl said.

"How did you know where the water came from?" Edna asked.

"I know the smell of Lost River," Bog Girl said, and she looked directly into my face, then Frannie's, as if daring us to tell them about our afternoon in the story of Hamelin.

There was a knock at the door and a woman the age of our mother, awash in tears, had left a wagon outside, carrying the bodies of her three daughters. Our father nodded to Bog Girl, who followed him out to the barn. Our mother poured cream and sugar over our peaches and, though she would not eat the peaches, Lucy drank the cream; the minister folded our father's list beside his dinner plate and his wife wiped the corn from his beard with her napkin.

"The flu is terrible this year," Edna said.

"Would you like coffee?" our mother asked the minister.

"We should be getting back," the minister said.

Lucy, licking cream from her spoon, began to hum and her humming reminded me of Bog Girl's music in the forest, and of rivers rushing through valleys, of rivers where salmon swam upstream every spring, on their way to eggs and death, and of the river in Hamelin, where the rats and the children danced behind the Piper, lost in a trance, a cold current carrying them out of their village, and away from the mountains which turned blue each evening, away from cobblestone alleyways, and blankets, and crumbs, and fireplaces.

Chapter Fourteen

It was sunny and the wind blew from the east on the first day of the carnival. Each spring, the Irish Travellers of Darkesville gathered with their friends and relations from far away, near the train stop, to play music and tell fortunes; they drove their caravans, painted red, purple, and blue, and erected their tents, which rippled and billowed in the wind. This carnival was one of the reasons why Josie and Helen had settled a mile from Great Aunt Nora's house. It was what brought Jasper to Louisa long ago. The Scarboroughs had wandered, all through Helen and Josie's early childhoods, a dog with a narrow face and thin legs following in their wagon tracks. Then, their parents found the Darkesville Carnival, where they made enough money to settle down, and build a house at the edge of the Clotho forest. Each spring, wealthy vacationers took trains to the Blue Ridge mountains to stay in inns with wraparound porches, and soak themselves in mineral springs. They hiked, and rode horses, and took tea, and ate biscuits with blackberry jam in great rooms with stone fireplaces.

Along the way, they stopped at the Irish Carnival and paid to have their palms, cards, or tea leaves read; they paid to see Jasper and his cousins play their fiddles; they paid to see a pair of conjoined twins sing and tap dance; they paid for little cakes, or pots and pans, or dream catchers, or bead necklaces with lucky charms; they paid to sit in a dim room with a group of spiritualists, conversing with the dead.

Our father stayed home, in the barn. He had hired Ben McCoy, whose rain and sewing machine repair businesses were faltering, to build Clotho coffins with him. Our mother and Beatrice brought us to the carnival, our mother driving our dark horses through the meadow and over the winding dirt roads that led to the village, which was built into the side of North Mountain. Ariel's hands on the reigns were so precise the horses understood her perfectly; she wore a Poiret Gray Suit; we drove past the country store with its wide front porch, and Dr. Saunders' office in a low building with a tin roof, past the mill and train depot, past the hammering of the blacksmith, and the monument to the Revolutionary War dead. Our mother stayed with the horses, their velvet ears twitching under the shade of a tree, with a book about herbs and a pair of baby booties she was knitting; she gave us each twenty cents.

"I'll keep your cape for you, if you're hot," our mother said to Bog Girl.

"I'm not hot," Bog Girl said.

We were supposed to visit Louisa's caravan; then, Frannie and I were going to spend a few hours walking around the carnival itself with Helen and Josie. Frannie had been given our father's watch, which hung from a chain, and she pulled that fat silver

watch out of her sweater pocket frequently, checking the time, though I think she was also admiring
its beauty, and the fact that she had been chosen as
our timekeeper. Beatrice looked frightened and she
took hold of Lucy's hand; Lucy held onto Bog Girl,
and we walked past tables of decorated cakes and
fruit pies, past the rippling tents which seemed to
contain laughter and color and music. At the edge
of the high grass, in a ring of caravans, we found
Louisa, the sign on her door reading: *Louisa Scarborough, Fortune Telling and Palmistry*. We knocked and
waited a few minutes, watching families unfold their
blankets and open their baskets to dine beneath the
Weeping Willow trees. After a moment the door to
the caravan swung open, and Helen led us down a
narrow passage, past a miniature kitchen, to a room
at the back, lit with candles, where Louisa presided
over a table. She wore many rings on her fingers
that glittered in the low light. It took a moment for
our eyes to adjust to the twilight of the Scarborough
caravan. I remembered how Josie and Helen had
shown Frannie and me the inside of this caravan the
winter we first moved to Darkesville; our parents
were talking about dull things with their parents
in the parlor, and Josie and Helen had summoned
us outside: the heavy, ornate key to the caravan in
Josie's pocket. They had shown us how it was possible to carry your house through the world like a
turtle, had shown us where they ate and slept during
the years when they migrated, told us how they once
visited cities full of horses and hats, and caves in
deserts, how they had opened the back doors of the
caravan by the sea and let the breeze breathe over
them while they slept.

"I have milk and potatoes," Louisa said, smiling at Lucy and Bog Girl; Josie, who had been waiting for her mother's cue, brought these out on a tray.

"How long will you be needing them?" Beatrice asked.

"If they could stay three hours, I would pay them for their trouble," Louisa said.

"They're going to help you tell fortunes?" Beatrice said.

"They could try," Louisa said, giving Bog Girl her most luminous smile. It was the smile that caused Jasper Scarborough to comb his hair more carefully and ask Louisa to dance, the smile that Helen had Josie had both inherited but did not yet know how to use.

Bog Girl and Lucy were already drinking milk and making gestures to one another with their hands. One gesture, which they repeated, looked like a spider with many legs.

"Could I stay?" Beatrice asked.

"People like *privacy* during these sessions," Louisa said. "You could wait in the kitchen."

"I'll make you a pot of tea," Helen said; a kitten followed closely at her heels, its movements round and soft.

"Could Helen and Josie walk around the carnival with us?" Frannie asked.

"If Beatrice would feel comfortable answering the door," Louisa said.

I thought Beatrice did not look particularly *comfortable* with the idea of answering the door, but she agreed, and we left her sitting stiffly in an alcove off the kitchen, wearing her maroon war crinolines at a table that folded down to become a bed. This was one of the things I loved most when Josie and Helen had first shown me the caravan: the transformation from night to day, how things folded away, or opened, and a kitchen became a bedroom, or a bench seat that was hollow inside became a closet. Van Beests loved transformations: a butterfly emerging from a chrysalis, a tadpole growing legs, night giving way to the first blush of dawn.

I wondered who would knock on Louisa's door and I wondered if Bog Girl or Lucy would divulge what they knew; it had occurred to all of us that Bog Girl knew things she would never reveal, that she could see without her eyes, and that her vision penetrated the darkness, the one that surrounded the plot of our own lives. I did not know whether Bog Girl could see how our father met our mother, while showing her caskets and tombstones after her brother Liam died, how they stood in a display room of the Van Beest Funeral Home where each polished coffin was opened, revealing a bed in the next world. I did not know if Bog Girl could see how Frannie and I had been born on an island ruled by tides where wild horses dug for water with their hooves. But I knew she could see the strange, glittering city of the future which was, for the rest of us, made of fog; I thought of Merlin, the wizard consultant to King Arthur in Camelot, and how his knowledge of the future weighed on him. He knew about, but could not prevent, Arthur's marriage to Guinevere, which would bring heartbreak, and the downfall of Camelot, just as Cassandra, in Greek myth, was licked by snakes in infancy, and uttered prophecies no one would believe, prophecies that could not deter murder or war. Louisa Scarborough could read signs: the sounds of owls before a sickness, or the meaning of a broken mirror. Small truths came to her in the shape of a tea leaf, or while following a map in a human palm. But Bog Girl and Lucy knew how all our stories ended; they knew what animals know when they run away before an earthquake or tsunami, the earth itself speaking to them in vibrations.

Frannie, Helen, Josie and I were glad to be released into the spring afternoon. Because Helen and Josie were Scarboroughs we were allowed to visit most tents for free; Helen and Josie knew the side entrances, where we parted the curtains and sat down in folding chairs, sometimes midway through an act or performance. In one tent we found a giant who never stopped growing, his head tilted to fit under the tent's gentle ceiling; he stood beside a dwarf, who was as small as Lucy, for he had quit growing before he was six months old. The giant and the dwarf were answering questions from the audience: *How do you find shoes that fit? How much food do you eat?* I wanted to stay there, listening to little-known facts, but Helen took us to a tent next door where a short, sweaty man with a shiny head had trained fleas; the fleas were arranged on tables, inside open suitcases and glass aquariums, and they wore thin, gold wires around their necks. They inhabited a miniature world in which they kicked balls, pushed carts up sandy hills, and rotated their own Ferris wheels; some appeared to play flutes and clarinets.

"How do you get them to do it?" Helen asked the man.

"If I revealed that, I'd be out of business, wouldn't I?" the man said.

Frannie and Josie and I leaned over the tiny worlds in which fleas ran a carnival of their own.

"Maybe they do it for food?" I guessed.

"What do fleas eat?" Josie asked.

"Blood," the sweaty man said.

In one scene, the fleas balanced on tightropes, and in another a single flea rode a unicycle while another pulled a carriage.

"How long do they live?" Helen asked.

"A few months," the man said. "I have to be training new ones all the time."

A woman in a voluminous dress, with four children holding onto her skirts, opened the tent, and dropped a few coins into the sweaty man's palm.

"Stand back," the man said to the children. "Do not touch."

"What happens if we touch?" the smallest child asked; she had been eating blue cotton candy and it was stuck to her cheeks.

"The fleas *bite*," the man said and the child with the blue cheeks took a step backwards, her eyes widening.

Outside the flapping fabric of the tent, on our way to buy lemonade and fried dough, Frannie, Helen, Josie and I argued about the fleas.

"It seems mean," Frannie said, "to enslave fleas."

"Fleas are dreadful," Josie said.

"Do you think he really *trains* them?" I asked.

"Look at that hat," Josie said, watching a big one with blue feathers float by.

"How does he avoid getting them all over his caravan?" Frannie asked.

We had joined the line for lemonade and fried dough which was being served through a window in a red caravan. Beside us, a tent with pictures of moons and stars repeated on its doors fluttered.

"What's that?" I asked.

"That's where the spiritualists hold their seances," Josie said.

"Our mother would approve," I said.

"Do you want to go?" Helen asked.

"Are we allowed?" Frannie asked.

"How many lemonades?" the woman behind the window asked.

We sat under a Weeping Willow tree, nibbling dough and drinking lemonade; behind us, I could hear a river slipping through the forest. I could hear children screaming as the carousel orbited. I heard a man outside the tent that contained the giant and the dwarf saying *Step right up and witness two of nature's miracles.*

"You might like the siamese twins," Josie said, licking powdered sugar from her fingers.

"They're stuck together?" I asked.

"Let's go to the seance," Frannie said. "We could ask about mom's dead brother."

"Uncle Liam?" I said; I thought of his portrait in a locket our mother sometimes wore around her neck, his drowned eyes as blue as the sea.

The dark curtains of the spiritualist tent parted and we stood up, brushing grass from our skirts; I watched Frannie check our father's pocket watch one last time, pulling on the chain: the face of time in her palm.

We were ten minutes into our seance when Bog Girl returned to us, chased by the wife of a tall man in a top hat who was sitting beside me, holding my hand a little too tightly. We had been arranged in a circle and a somber married couple were explaining to us about how the dead can send messages to the living; we were told to join hands, and use our energy to call forth our family ghosts. Then, the psychic, who wore a veil, began to compose messages on a chalkboard, the chalk itself ghostly against the starless sky of her board, and her husband read these aloud to us. *Sell the cattle and the house* the first message read and we were asked to consider whether that message might be for us. Frannie tugged at my sleeve and I could feel that she was trying to contain her laughter in the shadowy dusk; I wanted to decipher the expressions on the faces of Helen and Josie but found I could not.

"Paul?" a woman's voice called, and I thought at first that a ghost had arrived to address us all. "Paul?" the voice said again.

The tall man beside me stood up, dropping my hand. "Mother?" he said.

"No," the voice said, growing closer, "it's me, your wife."

"But my wife isn't dead," Paul said.

"No, I am most certainly *not*," the wife said, "at least not yet."

I saw Bog Girl run around our table then, her blue cape flapping behind her, and a woman with her hair pulled back in a severe bun appeared to be *chasing* her.

"Paul," the wife said, "we have to leave now."

"I thought you were having your tea leaves read," Paul said.

"This girl with a cape told me I'm going to *die*," the wife said. "She said we're all going to die."

"We will, eventually," Paul said. "I'm trying to talk to my mother."

"We need to make a safe space for the dead to speak," the veiled psychic said, her chalkboard trembling.

"Why bother," the wife said, "according to the girl in the cape we're going to join them quite soon."

I thought of the warnings on gravestones in the Methodist cemetery: *as I am so you will be* and *it's later than you think.* I watched Bog Girl run out of the tent, past the caravan full of dough and lemonade, parting the limbs of the sweeping forest trees.

Chapter Fifteen

I can tell you how each of us got sick. Frannie was first, complaining of a headache a few days after the carnival while our father was reading us the story of Rapunzel, whose mother craved lettuce from a witch's garden; Frannie held her hand against her throat while Bog Girl and our father took turns reading the fairy tale aloud. Angry over stolen lettuce, the witch in the story pilfered the pregnant woman's baby, named her Rapunzel, and raised the girl in a tower without stairs or doors; Rapunzel's hair was flung out a window and used as a rope; in my dreams, our meadow filled with bulbous heads of lettuce, and all the lettuce grew eyes.

When I woke, in the morning, Frannie was too cold to come downstairs and eat; her back was turned to me, and her teeth chattered; our quilts had gathered around her so my own legs were exposed; we often argued with our quilts at night, each of us tugging. I walked down the hallway, into our parents' bedroom, where our mother sat at her desk writing something that I thought might be a list. Our mother liked to make lists and fold them until they were small in her pockets.

"Frannie is too cold to eat breakfast," I said.

Ariel stood up and walked past me, her pen fainting.

Bog Girl and I ate our breakfast together; she sat on her bed between Gossamer and Speck, her glass of milk luminous in the morning light, and I sat at the table, cutting my blueberry pancake into pieces, drowning each bite in syrup. Bog Girl was reading books she brought in with her from the barn after the carnival, books with stories so strange our father had not yet read them aloud to Frannie and me. One was called *Dracula* and showed a dark creature, in a hat, on the cover. The other was called *Frankenstein* and concerned a monster.

"Are those books *scary*?" I asked Bog Girl.

"I like them," Bog Girl said.

Father came in from the barn and began brewing coffee on the stove.

"Vampires can't stand light?" Bog Girl asked.

"They don't like garlic either," our father said.

"Frannie has a fever," our mother said, appearing at the base of the stairs.

"She was saying something about her throat last night," our father said.

"What are vampires?" I asked.

"They are both dead and undead," Bog Girl said.

"Like you?" I asked.

"Anne, come here; let me feel your forehead," our mother said.

"I don't *feel* sick," I said.

"I'm going to call Dr. Saunders," our father said.

"Tell him Frannie can't get out of bed," our mother said.

"We shouldn't have gone to the carnival," I said.

"I didn't want to tell anyone about their future," Bog Girl said.

"Can you connect me to Dr. Saunders' office?" our father asked the operator.

Dr. Saunders did not arrive until evening because there were so many sick people in Darkesville. By the time he knocked on our front door the day was growing dim, our clocks and vases in silhouette, no longer casting shadows. Bog Girl answered because she was the only healthy member of our household. Dr. Saunders carried his black bag and half of a turkey sandwich that he had been trying, unsuccessfully, to eat all afternoon. He placed this sandwich on my bedside table when he listened to my lungs. Ben McCoy was working in our barn, where the bodies of children had begun to arrive, and Bog Girl told him how to store them in peat. McCoy took breaks frequently and stood behind the barn, smoking, one hand in his pocket, his flat cap pulled low. Slowly, the fate of Darkesville unfolded just as Bog Girl predicted at Louisa's fortune telling table. Louisa told our mother Bog Girl had been mute during the first couple of fortune telling sessions: one in which a pregnant woman wanted to know whether her unborn child was male or female, and one in which a man wanted to know how to invest his money. Louisa and Ariel sat together on our porch, after the carnival, and I could hear them through my bedroom window.

"After the man left, I told Lucy and Bog Girl they could help people if they would just *say what they knew*," Louisa said, "and they did help a young girl who was trying to decide between two suitors."

"What did they say?" our mother asked.

"They told the girl that one man seemed kind and the other seemed gruff, but their true selves were hidden, and not what they appeared to be," Louisa said. "I encouraged Bog Girl, because I thought she had done well; I told her she might have prevented an unhappy union."

"So, she told the next woman she was going to *die*?" our mother asked.

"She told her that her husband did not love her," Louisa said, "and that her son was a thief. Then, she told her none of this mattered because she, and most people she knew, would be dead in a few days," Louisa said.

"No wonder that woman chased her out of your caravan," our mother said, laughing. I loved when our mother laughed: her head flung back, the delicate stalk of her neck exposed.

Once, at a funeral for a child, when I was small, my father pointed out to me how the friends who came to console the grieving mother did not seem to know *they* were going to die. They brought flowers and casseroles and stood around the casket dreaming of their own futures, which seemed as vast as the sea. Our father taught Frannie and me that death and life are intertwined like fire and air, or earth and water; he showed us the inscription on the grandfather clock behind our piano which said *night soon*.

If you had asked me during that fever whether or not I was going to die I would have said I could feel death leaning over me, could hear the wind shift in the Clotho trees outside; I dreamed of Lost River: its depths, and eddies, and vascular boundaries, and I dreamed of the bog growing heavy and wet. I dreamed of a cave full of cats where Gossamer held his tail in the shape of a question mark. I was aware of Dr. Saunders touching my chest with his icy stethoscope, and I was aware of Frannie in the bed beside me, her skin burning. I knew somehow that Dr. Saunders had taken up drawing as a hobby, that he stood sometimes in his yard, trying to sketch a pond in his garden where fish swam, immersed in the liquid silence of a sunken world. I was aware of Speck moving in and out of our window, the smell of evening in his fur.

While I was fevered I dreamed of the day Frannie and I were fishing with our grandfather Willem Van Beast, our lines cast off the dock behind his mortuary on the North Carolina island of our early childhood, when a telegram arrived. This was the place where both of our parents had grown up: a land of sand dunes and coves and tides, a kingdom of cypress trees and mosquitoes; here our great-grandparents and aunts and uncles learned to rake for clams, and salvage cargo from shipwrecks, and weather hurricanes; they motored through lagoons on boats, paying attention to the tides, and rode the wild horses that had been cast off Spanish ships in the static horse latitudes, to lighten the load. I remembered how the dark man delivering the telegram had been a friend of our grandfather's in grade school and they stood together, at the edge of the dock, discussing a particularly strict teacher they had suffered under in third grade, remembering her ruler on their knuckles. Our grandfather tore open the envelope just as Frannie caught an eel on her line so, for me, the news that Great Aunt Nora had died—the news that would eventually bring our family to North Mountain, in Darkesville—will always move like a creature that is half snake, half fish. I dreamed, too, of the summer day that Frannie and I had been playing in the loft of the barn and come across the paintings of Great Aunt Nora. She had favored oil paints and had a vaguely Impressionist style; each of her colossal canvases explored a landscape that was now familiar to Frannie and me: The Clotho forest, Lost River, the bog, a sheltering cave to the east of our Methodist cemetery. If you looked closely, you could see Nora's dead husband, Jack, wandering at the edges of each canvas: a small, pointy dog at his feet, his face rendered in profile, squinting into the middle distance. In dreams I watched as an old gypsy widow burned her late husband's love letters in a meadow that became our Clotho forest, each ember of her lost love like a seed. I found myself at a table of ghosts who were eating winter instead of food.

I heard the voice of Mr. McCoy and the sounds of horses' hooves; I heard doors opening and closing. I dreamed of Bog Girl among ghosts in the Clotho forest. The first time I woke for a couple of hours I could hear feet on the stairs and Bog Girl appeared at my bedside with a bowl of potato soup. She had a strange, heavy-set woman with her, carrying pitchers and buckets. I wondered where Bog Girl had found someone to help her in town, where everyone was too sick to lift their heads, but I learned later that this woman, Sylvia, had come from the forest itself, that Bog Girl had discovered her drinking from Lost River and brought her home so she could warm

Chapter Sixteen

When Frannie and I went to school at our kitchen table our father set out the calendar with its names for months and days. We practiced writing the date on our slates before each assignment. Frannie liked writing the numbers but I liked the names and the poem we were given to help us remember: *Monday's child is fair of face; Tuesday's child is full of grace; Wednesday's child is full of woe; Thursday's child has far to go; Friday's child is loving and giving; Saturday's child works hard for a living; And the child that is born on the Sabbath Day is bonny and blithe and good and gay.* Frannie had been born on a Tuesday: graceful as she climbed into the canopies of our trees, but I was born on a Thursday and my destiny was full of distances. Here, though, on the island of sickness, all names and numbers receded, each day achy and vague.

One night, a Saturday I would later learn, I woke and I was no longer cold; I felt hungry. Frannie was tucked in beside me, her honey hair damp against her pillow. The house was quiet though I could hear the wind rearranging the snow outside. I descended, carrying a candle, my shadow rising beside me, and found Bog Girl and Sylvia in the parlor, their noses pressed against window glass. They were counting the bodies that had appeared on our doorstep, their limbs lost to drifting snow; here and there you could make out a foot or hand or a bit of hair disappearing into white. They spoke with their hands, gesturing silently as Lucy and Bog Girl did, except Bog Girl was using only one hand now, her other wrapped in a bit of scrap cloth from the quilting closet: a skirt from a dress I had outgrown. I liked the way our cloth had many lives and shapes: rising and falling away as dresses, aprons, curtains, tablecloths, quilts.

"Is all of Darkesville dead?" I asked.

"What are you doing out of bed?" Sylvia said, and I could tell she had once been a mother: the worry line between her eyes permanently creased. Sylvia had projects scattered around our house and I came to know her, in those weeks, as a woman who started many things but finished nothing: a mitten half-knitted on the table, vegetables half-chopped for a soup, our fire burning low.

"Is McCoy in the barn?" I asked.

Gossamer rose from some distant corner and threaded herself between my legs, her fur as soft as sleep. I could hear the grandfather clock in the corner swinging the pendulum of time. I felt suddenly tired and Bog Girl returned me to bed with a bit of jam and bread and a cup of tea. I warmed myself beside Frannie and watched Speck arrange three socks in a corner of the room until they became a nest. Bog Girl blew out my candle. She was wearing one of my old house dresses and I liked imagining her as my doppelgänger, tending our family as I rested. She was the part of me that stayed awake while I was asleep, the part that already knew what would happen next. When I was not jealous I liked watching her learn to read with our father; she resembled me so watching her was like watching myself.

When I woke again it was to the sound of our mother calling out; Frannie and I lifted our heads; Frannie's hand reached for mine and I understood that she was cool now, that the moonless light of morning was leaking through our windowpanes. We heard the sound of feet on the stairs, the low voice of McCoy, the banging of a pot. This was the day our father would die, but we didn't know that yet. Bog Girl would teach me that knowing is terrible and useless, that the future is a fixed thing: the script of a play that will always have the same ending, a map to a strange country where your ship will dock no matter which way you steer beneath the stars. We were like Sleeping Beauty, who would always prick her finger on a spinning wheel no matter how many her father burned at the center of town, like Oedipus who could not avoid killing his father and marrying his mother. Bog Girl believed she would always fall into the bog, in every version of her story, that there was no rendering in which she rode through our forest with her family and returned to Pennsylvania or Ohio, where a grandmother was cooking a roast and a dog waited beneath a porch.

McCoy and Bog Girl had taught Sylvia to feed the horses which she had managed during the worst hours of our illness. The trail worn by her big feet moving across snow was marked by a rope McCoy tied to our front porch and extended all the way to the horse barn so she would not get lost. On her last run, the day before, Sylvia had served the oats and corn, and broken the ice over the horses' water buckets, but had forgotten to secure the gate as she was leaving, and now our mother called out because she had seen the two mares frolicking outside, the black velvet of their ears twitching in the falling snow, their breath steaming. Throughout our father's dying McCoy and Bog Girl took turns in the drifting snow trying to lure the horses back to their stalls with lumps of sugar.

Dying is different when it happens to someone you love. Our mother says it is the same with childbirth, which also takes place regularly but is never ordinary. In each case a veil lifts, or a passage opens; the space between worlds grows thin. We all know this and yet, it seems, we do not. Throughout our father's dying the animals gathered, full of their wordless knowing. There were wild Spanish horses on the island we came from in North Carolina and they were known to sleep beneath the cottages of people under duress; they gathered under the floorboards of women whose husbands would not return from the sea, and they gathered under the bedrooms of children with Scarlet Fever. Speck ran along the headboard of our parents' bed in the late afternoon and tucked himself under our father's pillow. Gossamer leapt onto the bed in the evening, when our father's breathing rattled, and curled up at his feet. By the end, Bog Girl and Frannie and Mother and I were on the bed too. Our father seemed to float away though his body was before us: his dark eyelashes pressed against his cheeks, the hands that loved to turn the pages of books and open a chocolate bar as empty as they had been at his birth. It was Sylvia who noticed that the horses had gathered beneath the window of our parents' bedroom: their noses pressed to window glass, their dark manes rippling.

Chapter Seventeen

Frannie and Bog Girl and I knew at once that we must bring our father back; Ariel had fallen against her pillows and she would not rise again for some time. McCoy went out to return the horses to their barn, and Bog Girl and Sylvia wanted to carry our father to a coffin he made for himself and kept in his office in the barn.

"Couldn't we keep him here a while longer?" our mother asked, refusing to let go of his hand.

"Not if we mean to revive him," Bog Girl said.

"I hate thinking of him out in the cold," our mother said.

"The cold is inside him now," Bog Girl said.

I thought of my father's veins filling with winter, his absence inside each of us like night.

Frannie and I were weak from coughing and the wind outside pierced our coats. We passed bodies everywhere: some of them children we had played with at birthday parties, or women who had attended quilting bees in our parlor, some of them strangers lost to a deep and permanent frost. I found it hard to imagine what would be left of our town when the flu ran its course. Who would sort the mail, and who would deliver the milk, and who would plow the fields, and who would forge the shoes for our horses? Frannie and I stood over Fergus' desk full of notes and tried to locate the formula he had settled on for resurrecting the dead. It was there, in his barn, among his papers, touching the inelegant scratch of his handwriting from a fountain pen, that I realized how lost I was without him. I did not want to read books without hearing his voice; I didn't want to open the barn door and find only cats. Here, too, bodies were stacked up the way McCoy must have left them before he was too ill to go on. I knew the houses of Darkesville were full of people lost in blizzards like our own: unable to understand the new geography of their lives, everything familiar disappearing under heavy snow. Our cats rearranged themselves in the hay, and on coffins, and a willowy one slept on our father's desk, her purr like the motor of a boat on our distant childhood island.

"Do you think we could go back in the house?" Frannie asked and I looked up from the notebooks to see how pale she was.

"We can read in front of the fire," I said.

Inside, Sylvia stood over a pot of potato soup, stirring, and our mother was upstairs, deep in her bed, crying. Our house was like the descriptions we read in the newspaper of rescued widows and orphans aboard the Carpathia, after the Titanic went down: that eerie aftermath of survivors in ruined smoking jackets and evening gowns, pointed towards New York harbor in a light rain. McCoy returned from the horse barn and he and Bog Girl stood on the porch, discussing the accumulating bodies to the sound of a carriage arriving, bringing more. I stirred the fire, felt myself growing faint. Sometimes our telephone rang and McCoy answered it saying *Van Beest residence,* which made us sound strange and formal; I did not like the idea of being a Van Beest without our father.

"We need to get peat and cut down a Clotho tree," Frannie said, going through our father's notes. "We're going to need water from the Lost River and Ghost Pipe and I don't know what we'll do about the weather." She paused to cough.

"We have to bring him back," I said, feeling tears rise at the back of my throat.

We ate and slept badly and loaded the wagon in the morning. Only Bog Girl and I were well enough to make the journey. We left McCoy to handle the rising tide of the dead, and Sylvia to tend Ariel and Frannie, who now shared a bed. I looked at the similar oval of their faces, the green eyes and honey hair. I thought of that bed which Frannie and I had visited all through childhood in the middle of the night, the bed where we found the comfort of our mother and father entwined; then, I forced myself not to think of it.

Bog Girl and I were passing Lost River and this is where I first saw them: a flock of ghosts at the banks, just as Great Aunt Nora had painted them, drinking from their cupped hands, some of them seated around a table fashioned from snow. They were translucent and they moved as animals move when they have been disrupted: like a herd of deer leaping into obscurity, flicking the whites of their tails, or a murmuration of starlings rising as one seamless shroud from a field. I remembered Great

Aunt Nora's dead husband, Jack, drinking from the river in her letter and I wondered if he was still here, among the earthly dead. I wondered what drew the dead to our forest and why they lingered at the edge of our lives like moths. I knew what I wanted from the dead—to see or speak to them—but I did not know what they wanted from me. Bog Girl handed me the horses' reigns and descended to the river, her cape rising behind her. She made a high musical sound, blowing into her hands, that caused the ghosts to gather. The ghosts reminded me of the fireflies on our lawn in June, eluding our glass jars, of the fog that sometimes wrapped North Mountain in forgetfulness. They could smell the other world on Bog Girl's cape and skin; they touched her dusky hair and joined hands and began to dance in a circle around her. I could see Bog Girl's face, though more snow had begun to fall, slanting in the wind, and she was as luminous as a tree that has burst into blossom.

"Do you *know* those ghosts?" I asked when she returned to the wagon.

"I do," she said.

"How?" I asked.

"They came to me, years ago, in the bog," she said.

I tried to picture seasons passing in the dark peat, where Bog Girl waited the way Rapunzel waited for freedom. I remembered how Louisa had told me a story, the summer before, of a gypsy woman who fell in love with a ghost who could only appear to her at night, an Irish Traveller who turned away from the world of the living: her roof leaking, her fields fallow.

Presently, the Scarborough house came into view and I saw a plume of smoke rising from their chimney, and was filled with hope. Then, I caught sight of a new litter of dachshund puppies Louisa had been breeding, running into the yard through a hole in the barn, and I knew Louisa must be sick because I had never known her to allow such new creatures to run among the predators in our forest. Bog Girl tied up the horses, and I picked up the puppy I could catch: a black and tan with a pointed, slender nose I carried to the front door of the Scarborough house, where I was met by Helen, who had been crying. I slipped the dog into her arms and we hugged each other with the puppy between us, its tail twitching as rhythmically as a heart.

"Are you alone?" I asked, for at first I could see no one else.

"I'm here," Jasper said, coughing beneath a quilt on a couch beside the fire. "We're going to need your father's help."

"He can't help," I said.

"Dear God," Jasper said.

"Is Josie upstairs?" I asked.

Helen began to weep again, the puppy wiggling so fiercely that she released him.

"We lost Josie and Louisa last night," Jasper said.

I thought of Josie and Louisa lost in a deep wood where all the trees looked alike, pebbles in their pockets.

Bog Girl appeared behind me, two brown dachshunds at her heels; they tumbled over one another, began sniffing the head of my black and tan.

"Josie and Louisa need to be moved someplace cold," Bog Girl said.

How long, I wondered, had she known our friends were dead?

"We were worried about wild animals," Helen said, her face revealed by so much crying. "How can *I* be the one who lived?"

I understood what she meant. I always thought our father would live to be an old man but imagined our mother was delicate. I didn't know yet that death would come the way you don't imagine, preferring surprise.

"We can't revive them if they're too decomposed," Bog Girl said. "We're on our way to gather peat."

"Do you know how to bring them back?" Jasper asked.

"We have my father's notes," I said.

"I could chop down Clotho trees, for the coffins," Jasper said.

The puppies rolled in front of the fireplace; one of the brown ones bent low to pee on a rug. I thought of how carefully Louisa kept the house, about how she would never have allowed these new puppies in the living room. I thought of how the rules we all lived by were suspended now that the dead outnumbered the living.

"You stay here," Bog Girl said to me. "Get the bodies ready to travel; I'll go to the bog."

I nodded, grateful to be left with Helen and Jasper in a warm living room, with puppies. I noticed that Bog Girl had grown older without growing taller, that she walked with authority to the dark horses waiting in the yard, their breath spectral in the morning light.

Chapter Eighteen

The snow began again, filling the air with white as we loaded the bodies of Louisa and Josie into Jasper's wagon. Snow made alabaster cornices at the edge of the jockey box. Bog Girl had gathered a dozen buckets of peat but I could see that her left hand really troubled her now, its fingers dark with numbness; Jasper had cut down a few Clotho trees and they were stacked in the back of our wagon like silent, fallen giants; we rode in a procession through the ivory forest which reminded me of a cathedral. Helen brought two of Louisa's puppies in a crate with a quilt; she kept the black and tan in her lap, its warmth a comfort to her slender hands.

Bog Girl drove our horses out of the forest and I caught sight of Sylvia, her curly hair tied up in a scarf, in our yard, arranging bodies in rows like vegetables in some corporeal garden; I could see from her tracks through the snow that she had also been wandering towards Lost River, perhaps to drink forgetfulness from her cupped hands, or maybe to visit the ghosts from her past. Bog Girl must have asked her to gather herbs for I could see she had Ghost Pipe hanging from her pockets. How, I wondered, had Sylvia come back to this life without our father to put her in peat, and bless her with river water and Ghost Pipe, and place her in a Clotho coffin? Where had Bog Girl found her? How many more were like her, drifting through Darkesville on their way to errands I did not understand?

While Bog Girl tied up the horses I ran upstairs to check on Frannie and my mother. I found them sleeping with their arms entwined like vines, Speck nested between their heads. When he saw me, Speck darted up the headboard and cleaned his face with his hands. Helen called to me from the hall-way where her black and tan puppy leapt from her arms and leaned its front paws against the bed, its tail moving in circles. Speck made a chittering sound when the dachshund hopped onto the quilts, his exit to the next room full of disapproval, his tail flicking hostilities, and Frannie's eyes were licked open by the puppy, who knew only warmth and curiosity, his whole, low body writhing with life. Helen reached her hand to hold Frannie's while our mother, still sleeping, rolled over, her breathing raspy.

"Anne?" Bog Girl called and I hurried downstairs, holding my skirt in one hand; I was aware that my skirt was wrinkled, and my shirt was dirty, and my mother was too sick to correct me; I longed for her solid precision and rigidity, longed for her to spit on her finger and clean my cheek, longed for her to make a good dinner and spend the meal asking my father whether it could be better. Bog Girl led me to the barn where McCoy and Jasper were nearly finished fashioning coffins from Clotho trees; Jasper was fixing the hinges while McCoy sanded the sides. I caught sight of Louisa and Josie laid out on a table in the corner, still in the nightgowns they had worn to bed the night before, not knowing it would be their last night dwelling as a family in their drafty house at the edge of the Clotho forest. I saw my father in his coffin and it was his hands that made me cry: unable to open books or chocolate bars or take notes at his desk: my father who taught me about the dead had joined them, leaving behind his armchair and pipe for the silent acres of the afterlife.

"I need you to fill the coffins with peat," Bog Girl said, touching her left hand tenderly with her right. "We should get them to the church before nightfall."

"What about the weather?" I asked, listening to the wind.

"We'll have to hope it doesn't matter," Bog Girl said.

Sylvia opened the barn door, a glass of milk in her hand, and she and Bog Girl took turns sipping from it. It looked to me as if they were drinking winter itself: swallowing the white cold. They stood together as Bog Girl had often stood with Lucy, in a huddle from which I was excluded.

It was evening before we were ready to make our procession to the church. This might have been one of our father's funerals but he was not driving the horses. We left behind Helen, and Frannie, and my mother, and Sylvia, and McCoy, so only Jasper and Bog Girl and I made the journey. I was so tired, but I did not want to leave anything about my father's resurrection to chance. During these days I would travel several times through our forest, beside Lost River, and on each expedition I felt the kingdom of

the dead expanding, their chilly eyes watching. I
suppose you could say that Bog Girl and I got into
an argument after we arrived at the church, where
we found the minister, George, weeping over the
body of his stout wife, Edna. She had collapsed in
the chapel upon seeing ghosts, while kneeling at
the altar. The minister thought she was dead—they
had both been fevered and coughing for days—but
Bog Girl knew at once that she had only fainted and
Jasper, with some effort, lifted her corpulent body
over his shoulder and carried her to a bed in the
rectory.

"Edna?" the minister said, when his wife's eyelids
fluttered. She was sprawled inelegantly over their
quilt.

"I saw *ghosts*," she said.

"We need keys to the cellar," Jasper said.

"You saw *angels*," the minister said.

"She saw ghosts," Bog Girl corrected.

"We're going to need someplace to stay the
night," Jasper said.

My fight with Bog Girl began in the cellar, where
we were arranging the bodies in their Clotho coffins
and weaving Ghost Pipe into their hair; Jasper had
left Josie with her favorite hat, and Louisa with her
Tarot cards, and disappeared upstairs for the night,
and the minister had offered his brief blessing
before hurrying away to tend his wife. Bog Girl and
I touched each forehead with water from the Lost
River—Louisa, Josie, Fergus—and were standing
together in the windowless hush. I suppose I wanted
to be standing with Frannie, who was too sick to
leave our parents' bedroom, wanted my *real* sister
beside me instead of this girl who resembled me but

was not my true relation. I did not feel love from Bog Girl, only impatience and a sense of duty.

"Is he coming back?" I asked her.

"I don't want to talk about it," Bog Girl said.

"I need to know," I said.

The future isn't what you think," Bog Girl said, "it isn't a fixed place; it's just a place."

"What does that mean?" I said. "Where did you find Sylvia?"

"I needed *help*," Bog Girl said.

"Can you bring people back?" I asked.

"Sylvia was in the bog," Bog Girl said, "like I was."

"I want my father," I said.

"He's right here," Bog Girl said, touching his black hair.

"He's gone," I said.

"There is so much you can't see," Bog Girl said.

"What's wrong with your hand?" I asked.

Bog Girl did not reply.

"Can you die again?" I asked.

"You're tired," Bog Girl said.

"I could sleep," I said, "if you would tell me what's going to happen."

"You won't sleep," Bog Girl said, and she left me down there, in the cold, with the dead: Josie as shrouded as she had been that day we played Hide and Seek and she could not be found, Louisa inert in the coffin Jasper had carved from our forest of ghosts, my father eclipsed.

Chapter Nineteen

Bog Girl was right, of course, that I could not sleep. I collapsed on a pew in the church, near a stained glass window that showed Jesus with his eyes closed, his limbs pinned by nails. Time was so slow that it felt as if minutes became seasons; I rose at first light to the sound of the minister's wife, Edna, yelling and swatting the air with a broom. A bat was troubling the rafters and Edna was now fully revived after her night of sound sleep. She was balanced on the pew adjacent mine, raking the air as a winged creature swooped low then high. I stood up, shaking my rumpled skirt, and was looking around for Bog Girl or Jasper, when I saw my father wandering down a hallway, holding Josie's hand.

"Papa!" I said, elated, my heart fast, but he stood rigidly, his eyes moving over me as they might move over a stranger.

"It's me, Anne," I said, and I saw a trace of recognition in his eyes; I will remember that intimation forever. Josie tilted her head, her velvet Tudor beret waving a tall, wispy feather. She held more tightly to his hand.

"Josie," Jasper called, rising from a pew at the back of the church, "where is your mother?"

"I don't know if Josie can speak," I said.

"They need tea," Edna suggested, abandoning her broom and allowing the bat to waft back up into the rafters where, later, he would hang upside-down, gathering dust and time.

"Fergus," Jasper said. "Have you seen Louisa?"

My father took his pipe out of his jacket pocket but could not remember how to light it. He and Josie shivered and huddled together as if they were now kindred; they were disoriented and mute.

We returned to Orchard Ridge Road without Bog Girl or Louisa, both of whom had vanished; Jasper and I searched for their trails in the blowing snow, but the wind blew from the east, and snow drifted in great sheets over the thin slate stones of the cemetery; we could find no tracks. Edna and George agreed to go on searching and we rode away in our wagon, our horses hungry and cold, though we had covered them in blankets the night before. We stopped once beside Lost River so the horses could drink, dipping their dark heads into the river, and I saw no ghosts though it seemed as if the water was full of eyes; I felt the warmth of a gaze on my neck and turned to see a snowy owl turning its milky head. I felt I was an actor on a lit stage, the ghosts my audience.

It took weeks for my father's voice to return to him and, even so, it was not the wise storytelling voice that had gathered me close during my childhood. He seemed to be married to Josie instead of our mother and sat inelegantly at our kitchen table drinking milk and eating potatoes. He had forgotten how to read, his books abandoned, and he and Josie liked to warm themselves in front of our fire, their fingers jabbing the air with the sign language known only to the recently dead. Fergus and Josie both suffered from a lace-like rash that ran along their necks and wrists; our mother suggested that it might have been a reaction to Ghost Pipe.

"It's as if they have identical birth marks," Frannie whispered the first time we were alone in our bedroom together, with Speck scurrying along our headboard.

Like Bog Girl, Sylvia had vanished when we returned to Orchard Ridge Road, where there were so many fallen bodies the dead reminded me of the sand bags we used for hurricane flooding on our North Carolina island. McCoy had gone home, his deep footprints in the snow leading towards whatever was left of Darkesville. We found Helen and Frannie knitting in front of the fireplace, three intertwined dachshunds dozing at their feet, and Ariel upstairs, adrift in her quilts, guarded by Speck and Gossamer. Spring is, I suppose, the season of dampness and change and, as the snow melted, our altered world was revealed. There were immediate problems: trips to town to buy flour, or sugar, or eggs at the market where shelves were bare because the workers had been too sick to stock or make deliveries; the newspaper erupted in obituaries though there were too many dead for proper funerals. I tried to imagine how my father would have dealt with so many dead if he was still *himself.* In his new form, he liked to touch their arctic hands, or sit beside them, but showed no interest in burying them.

A commissioner in a starched uniform knocked on our door one Monday afternoon and told Fergus the bodies that had gathered on our property posed a health threat. I listened to his men arguing about whether or not the ground was too frozen for a mass grave. Then, a group of soldiers, recently returned from the war, put on face masks and lit the ground on fire to thaw it. The fire waxed and burned for most of the afternoon, while the stacked bodies of the dead waited. The soldiers thought they had put out the flames completely by nightfall, a circle of scorched earth steaming beyond our meadow, but embers tucked into the earth survived, and the wind blew them into the Clotho forest where they became hot seeds.

Chapter Twenty

The six fire horses of Darkesville had been trained to respond to a gong, and move quickly to a place in their stalls where harnesses would drop over them; they cantered down Orchard Ridge Road, pulling the pumper behind them. Frannie and I surfaced from our dreams to the sound of yelling and stood in our bedroom window, holding Speck, and watching a half dozen firemen spray water from hoses into a towering inferno, each Clotho tree traced in flames. The bodies of the dead caught fire too, stacked like firewood in the luminous night. A fireman knocked on our door, and spoke to our father about the danger, and our father stood rigidly, his face expressionless. The fireman said he would help us leave if the fire threatened our property; he was one of Fergus' friends, a man our father used to visit in town whenever he went to buy cloth or tobacco, but Fergus could not seem to remember how to make conversation, and our mother, who had, at last, risen from bed, tied on her apron and invited the fireman inside for coffee. The man removed his hat, ran a hand through his sweaty brown hair, and sat down at our kitchen table, watching the blaze through our window. A fire is a gorgeous thing if you are not afraid that it will consume you: rippling, hungry. The Clotho trees came alive with it even as they were ruined: their majestic leaves ardent as they fell. Van Beests have very bad luck mixed with very good luck my father once said, and so the wind blew to the south, away from Great Aunt Nora's crooked Victorian, and the fire did not rage across our lawn, or devour our carpets and lampshades, but, by dawn, it was smoldering ash and Lost River and the Scarborough house were revealed. They seemed naked, or stunned. It occurred to me then that there would be no more bringing the dead back to this world without Clotho trees for coffins, and Ghost Pipe to decorate bodies, and I wondered, of course, if some tunnel or veil to the afterlife had been burned up in our blaze as well. When I walked on the bare scorched earth, under a sky that seemed too obvious and low, I remembered the protective limbs of the Clotho trees, and the stories Frannie and I had enacted under their shade. I remembered the voices and laughter we'd heard in their crowns.

For weeks, Bog Girl, Louisa, and Sylvia were missing. Frannie and I found footprints in our meadow grass when we were hanging our laundry out to dry, the sleeves of our dresses gesturing in the wind, but the prints did not lead anywhere definitive, and they might have belonged to anyone. I felt sometimes, at night, in front of our fire, as if we were being watched and one day, in the basement fetching potatoes, I heard something rustling nearby, but this may have been a rat. Josie arrived on our porch, after walking through the ash of our missing forest at dawn, with the dachshunds nipping at her heels. She did not seem to remember Helen, or Frannie, or me, but was firmly attached to our father; she still loved hats but did not care whether or not they were fashionable. I saw her wearing one with fake fruit on top, and another that resembled Speck. She and our father liked to wait for the milk to be delivered in the early morning so they could drink it straight from the glass bottles. Our mother watched Fergus move through the house as if he were a stranger: his chocolate bars undisturbed in their wrappers, his hands not reaching for hers, or turning the pages of a story. We lost my father the first time when he died upstairs, the air of this world suddenly unbreathable, but we lost him again when he returned to us without his memory. No one besides McCoy knew that our father and Josie and Louisa had died so there was no fanfare about their return. They were like so many people who had been sick but rose up from their beds and were never quite the same.

All over Darkesville, people stayed home and avoided gatherings and once, on a rainy afternoon, when I held the phone to my ear, I heard the story of four women in Harpers Ferry who had gathered to play Bridge, all of them joking and wearing face masks. The flu must have been on their deck of cards, or already inside them for, two days later, they were all dead. I heard the story of two small children found alive in a house full of deceased adults: the pair discovered wandering in an open field, their faces sticky with jam, both of them guarded by a bulldog that showed his teeth when strangers came near. I learned that our sickness was *The Spanish Flu* by listening on our telephone to Dr. Saunders giving the numbers of the sick and dead in Darkesville to a man gathering data in a nearby city. I thought of that man—an insurance salesman maybe, or actuary, or scientist—sitting at a desk where people became variables in an equation. I learned that Dr. Saunders had caught the flu himself and nearly died. He attributed his survival to a medicine his wife, Mildred, concocted: honey and lemon and ginger and garlic and onions and hot peppers and chicken broth brewed together into a soup he was still sipping.

One late April day, Beatrice Mallicoat brought Lucy to visit and I saw that Lucy's left hand was tied up, as Bog Girl's had been.

"What happened?" I asked.

"She was building a snowman," Beatrice said, "and the cold seemed to get inside her fingers. They still bother her."

Lucy had been longing for Bog Girl, which was the reason for the visit, but she seemed happy enough to see Fergus and Josie, who spoke to her in their mutual sign language, and our mother packed a picnic in a basket, and we went out onto the lawn, to the edge of the burned earth where our Clotho forest should have been. We were eating ham biscuits, and potato salad, on a blanket, and talking about how strong the light had become without any trees. I had not known how much I loved having the light filtered by leaves, had not realized how much I preferred what was gentle and indirect: dappled shadows, shade.

"It's strange to have no forest," Beatrice said. "Everything looks bare."

"I didn't use enough lard in the biscuits," Ariel said.

"They're good," I told her, for our father remained silent; he no longer ate biscuits.

Frannie was feeding Speck a peanut and he took it in both hands, his two teeth nibbling. He had been disturbed by the forest fire and returned more quickly from his outings now, the scorched earth less appealing than the high branches. It was Speck who saw Bog Girl first, with her left hand still bandaged, parting the Blue Lupine in our meadow; a flock of the dead advanced behind her, watching her the way baby ducks watch their mothers. Speck scurried towards her and flicked his tail in greeting. I was glad to see Bog Girl again, striding as she had that day when she became the Piper and the wild animals recognized her power. Louisa was behind Bog Girl: her auburn hair shining, her dress unspoiled, and Josie ran to her, opening her arms. I saw Louisa tuck a strand of Josie's hair behind her ear; I noticed that Louisa had the same rash as Josie and our father: deep red, running down one side of her neck. They were all together now and it was easy to see that this was a new family, a tribe Ariel and Frannie and I did not belong to. Our mother averted her eyes when our father took Bog Girl's hand. Ariel was the first of us to understand that the dead were not really returning.

"Would you like some potato salad?" our mother asked Bog Girl.

Bog Girl knelt down at the edge of our blanket, her cape fluttering behind her, and Lucy dropped her cup of milk to kiss her.

"I'm sorry about the things I said in the church," I said.

"I can't stay," Bog Girl said.

The dead murmured and nodded behind her. I could not tell if they had died recently, of the flu, or if they had come up from the depths of the bog, or the cave. The dead had long hair and folded hands and a dewy, far-away look in their eyes.

"Are the ghosts gone?" I asked.

"Not entirely," Bog Girl said.

"Have you come for Lucy?" Beatrice asked.

"What is Sylvia doing?" Frannie asked, for we could see Sylvia opening our barn door, her curly hair blowing in the wind.

Bog Girl cupped her right hand and made a beautiful sound that might have come from a bird in another world, and a fox darted out of a den, and a flock of ravens descended from the sky, and landed on the shoulders of the dead, who gestured to one another in their own silent language. Sylvia emerged from the barn carrying a sack of potatoes, and she nodded to Bog Girl, who held Lucy with her right arm, and allowed our father to take her left. This was the last time Frannie and Ariel and I would see Fergus for a long time: his broad back turned to us, his bowler hat tilted jauntily on his head. And this was the third time we lost him: as he walked with Bog Girl through the acres where our magnificent forest once rose: that otherworldly grove with its roots reaching some other kingdom. The dead walked to the sound of Lost River rushing. We stood up, as if saluting, let our picnic blanket be lifted by the wind. I thought, at first, that Speck intended to travel with them, for he ran excitedly at their heels, but he came back to us after they had vanished beyond the horizon, while Beatrice and Frannie and I struggled to tuck our picnic back in its basket in the sudden cold gusts which came from the west. Speck returned to us, racing over the scorched earth, his two teeth chittering, his almond eyes peering into our tear-stained faces, bringing us news we could not understand.

Chapter Twenty-One

Our mother was a widow but not a widow. She slept alone on her side of the bed, leaving our father's side open, as if he might return. I caught her searching for him sometimes, in the barn, or walking beside Lost River, pretending to smoke his pipe. At dinner, once a week, she made lima beans for Fergus though none of the rest of us ate them. Ariel complained that grief made her stupid: too distracted to finish a task, sleepless, unhungry. Grief belongs to the living, who can remember the past but not see the future.

Without my father I struggled to find the stories that could serve as my map, my compass. I needed stories the way ship captains needed their sextants and constellations, the way palm readers needed the lines in a hand. Frannie and I read *The Odyssey* because the wife in the story, Penelope, waited as our mother did, sleeping in a bed that was also an olive tree, while her husband spent twenty years trying to return from a war. We read with Speck between us, and Gossamer in the corner, chewing his fur. We read a story in which a family was guarded by a mongoose that had nearly drowned in India: a mongoose who saved their son from the fangs of a snake. Without our forest, there was a clear, worn path between our house and the Scarborough house where Helen and Jasper had seen Louisa and Josie pass by after leaving our picnic: Josie's velvet hat blown off her head and alighting on their lawn. By May, Helen and Jasper decided to revive their old caravan and prepare it for travel. Helen said they had to replace the cushions and drapes which had been nibbled by mice; Jasper repainted the exterior with moons and stars and remade the kitchen so Helen could cook. Some summer evenings we gathered on our porch, and instead of listening to Louisa's ghost stories, we listened to Jasper playing a song on his banjo about a lonesome valley. Helen was sewing cushions, or learning to cook from our mother, who taught her to roll out biscuits with a rolling pin, flour sifting off the counter and onto the floorboards; she taught her to deep fry chicken in a cast iron frying pan. There was a part of the night when we all listened hard for our dead who might have been anywhere in the velvet shadows of North Mountain. I thought of them moving out there like the nocturnal animals: the bats and skunks and owls. Helen and Jasper brought the three dachshund puppies with them when they visited and they had named them Clotho, Lachesis, and Atropos, after the three fates. We knew when they were arriving or departing because the dogs preceded them in each direction: low-slung and short-legged, poking their slender noses down holes, searching for dens.

Frannie and I saw Bog Girl once when we were walking in the cemetery beside the Methodist church and again in late June, around my birthday, when I was teaching Frannie to swim in Lost River: arm over arm, her feet fluttering. In the cemetery, Bog Girl seemed to be visiting a grave, and she nodded to us before running behind the church and climbing a steep ravine. Frannie and I tried to follow but found ourselves caught in brambles and thorns: our skirts torn and our hands cut. When she appeared at Lost River we were floating downstream and she knelt at the edge, drinking. She seemed to wink.

"Your father says hello," she may have called, but the rushing water was so loud we could not be sure.

Frannie and I made a habit of visiting the bog at twilight, with Speck at our heels, and leaving little gifts of potatoes, or milk, or honey. These gifts vanished but we had no way of knowing whether they had been taken by the dead or the living. And when Speck died one late September day, his head too still in its nest of pillows, Frannie and I buried him in the bog, remembering how he had once fallen into our lives from the high branches of the Clotho forest. We hated our stagnant bedroom, the way nothing chittered, or flicked, or nibbled. We wondered if Bog Girl had found him, if she could still see everything, if she knew. We wondered if she was taking care of our father, if she loved him as we had. We wondered if she watched us through our windows, or thought of us at all. I remembered how she could see the glittering city of the future, but the past sank behind her: elusive and dark.

By October, when Helen and Jasper rode away in their caravan, waving to us as their horses pulled them beyond the horizon, Beatrice Mallicoat was pregnant. She came to lunch at our house each week, coat, and he liked to tell stories. Death brought us together as it had brought my parents together. Mick and I married when my mother grew frail and he moved into the house on Orchard Ridge Road, selling his newspaper business in Martinsburg. We tried to have a baby but could not, each month bringing blood instead of life. Then, in late winter, I vomited while shoveling a path to the barn and it seemed that a child had begun ticking inside me; I knew at once that she was a girl and that I would name her Irene, after my maternal grandmother, and I was well until my eighth month, which came in October, when I began having contractions and my bag of waters broke too soon. Ariel and Frannie helped me but my daughter arrived as I had: backwards, with a caul over her head, and she was small and did not want to breathe. Irene died as Lucy had and I remembered our mother bringing that bundle of stillness to our father so long ago: the way Lucy's face had reminded me of a soft apple. Irene had my father's hands and I insisted that we take her to the bog at first light the day after her birth though I was weak and the wind was sharp. Mick held my hand, and Frannie and David made a space in the peat, and we all left Irene there, wrapped in the dark brine that had nurtured Bog Girl. We went home to cover the mirrors, and stop the clocks, and speak with the bees, and grieve to the sound of our short dogs howling, to the music of David playing piano, and the teapot screaming in the afternoons. It was twilight when a knock came on our door, followed by the sound of crying, and when Mick answered he called for me and I rose up from the couch, where I had been wrapped in a quilt, warming my sorrow by the fire, and there was a basket woven from Clotho bark, and inside our daughter writhed in a web of Ghost Pipe, and her feet kicked, and she sucked her thumb. Mick and I looked out at the world of silhouettes— the barn, and mountains, and horses—and we saw them huddled together, at the edge of what was once our glorious forest, as if they were replacing the trees: Bog Girl, Lucy, my father, Louisa, and Josie in a new tea hat, returning the child who now belonged to both realms: my daughter of the living and the dead. When I rushed out to hug them they tried to speak to me with their hands, in that language I do not understand, and then they left me: a deep cold opening behind them, the kind that still causes me to shiver. And Mick and I had a tiny daughter, one who would never grow up to be a woman; we fed her on potatoes and milk with honey, and warmed her by the fire. We fed her stories of people playing music on the deck of the Titanic as it went down, and children raised by wild animals, stories of the Underworld where the dead drank forgetfulness and opened pomegranates, their fingers stained red. We found her in the meadow, sleeping with fawns, and near the barn, feeding blackberries to bears. And when she arrived we also discovered a single, slender Clotho tree in our meadow, drinking sunlight. Sometimes, when Irene could not sleep, we found her reading with her eyes closed; we knew she could see without her eyes, all the way to the end of the story, but we did not ask her to tell us what she knew. She had no proper birthday, having been born twice, and no age because she was both dead and alive. I remembered how jealous I had been of Bog Girl for stealing our father's attention, how sad I had been

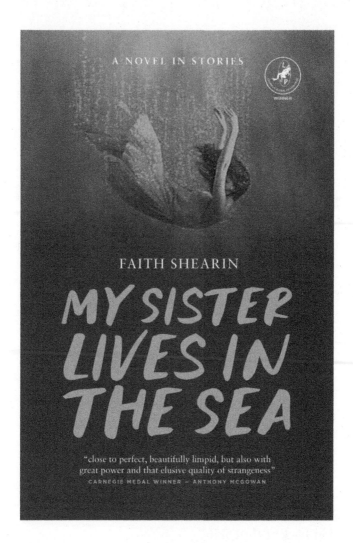

A NOVEL IN STORIES

FAITH SHEARIN

MY SISTER LIVES IN THE SEA

"close to perfect, beautifully limpid, but also with
great power and that elusive quality of strangeness"
CARNEGIE MEDAL WINNER — ANTHONY MCGOWAN

Coming next from Faith Shearin

The first chapter from her award-winning work:
My Sister Lives in the Sea

Appellations

When we checked into Big Meadows Lodge, we were given a new last name. Our father, Henry, has a thick southern accent, and when he called to make our reservation, he was misunderstood. According to the ski passes, and our tickets to the dining room, he was now Harry Bighorn.

"It's Henry Hawthorne," he said to a teenager with red hair and a disarray of stained teeth.

"It doesn't really matter," the teenager pointed out, "and it would take a while for the office to make new passes."

My sister, Beth, and I were surprised at how easy it was to become someone else.

"Bighorn?" our mother, Ruth, asked when we met her back at the cabin.

"The teenager at the front desk assured me that it doesn't matter," our father said.

"Can I introduce myself as Hazel Bighorn all week?" I said.

"Please don't," Beth said; she had stepped into the bathroom to comb the golden waterfall of her hair.

The day before, we'd left our coastal town in North Carolina and stared out the windows of our parents' station wagon as the roads grew narrow and nauseous; by the time we reached Big Meadows Lodge, we had passed a dozen lookouts where we were supposed to park and peer out at the Appalachian Mountains themselves, which could look hard and blue, or soft and green, depending.

Beth was excited to learn how to downhill ski with our father but I knew, without really knowing, that I would have trouble. Beth had always been more athletic than I was; at home, on our island, she joined the cross country team and, in the afternoons, she ran beside the ocean while I sat with a novel or sketchbook, watching. I was exhausted by the act of putting on my ski costume: the huge puffy pants with suspenders, the stiff boots that fit into skis so long I felt myself turning into a clown. In our first class, Beth learned to turn neatly from side to side while I hurtled, inelegantly, at a terrifying speed.

At lunch in the dining room, where we sat at a stern black table beneath a chandelier, I told my parents I did not want to spend the afternoon skiing.

"Beth is good at it, but I'm going to break something."

"You could go hiking with me," our mother said.

This is how my mother and I wound up on the Rose River Trail, following a scenic path that descended gently for two miles to a waterfall.

"I don't like to ski either," my mother said, once we were alone.

"Who could like it?" I said. "It's exhausting and dangerous."

We hiked in silence, the trees growing taller. I saw that my mother was worried by how few hikers we were passing.

"Maybe we should stop and rest?" she said, after we had gone a mile. We sat down together on a flat stone beside a place where the river argued with itself, then grew deeper.

"It seems to me," I said, "that our lives would be different if we were named Bighorn."

"Different in what way?"

"Wouldn't you want to be louder and more outgoing if you had a name like that?" I said. "Wouldn't we paint it in bright colors on our mailbox?"

"I didn't want to change my name when I got married," my mother said.

"Why not?"

"I couldn't see why your father's name should be more important than mine," my mother said, "and I liked the name Flynn. It reminded me of my red-haired father; people who heard it knew I was Irish."

This is when we heard the rustling, deep in the trees, when we glimpsed the face of a creature that might have been an ape or a bear. My mother and I sat still, our words half swallowed, and watched whatever it was turn its broad back to us and disappear into the afternoon's shadows.

At dinner we sat at a table marked with a silver *Bighorn* placard and my mother and I tried to describe what we had seen.

"It might have been a Bigfoot," I said.

"You mean Sasquatch," Beth said.

"They're the same thing, aren't they?"

"It was probably a bear," our mother said.

"Good evening, Bighorns," our waiter said when he delivered our menus, which featured sketches of forest wildlife: foxes, bobcats, deer, and wolves born from dark pencil lines.

The following afternoon, I was in our cabin, sitting in front of the fireplace and reading about spies, when I came to a chapter involving the exotic dancer Mata Hari; my book described how she dated military officers and politicians across Europe. I was squinting at a picture of her bra made of jewels, scarves draped over her shoulders, when Beth limped in, holding our father's arm.

"What happened?" I said.

"I ran into a tree," Beth said, hopping over to sit beside me on the couch. "I did something to my ankle."

"What are you reading?" Our father was eying the pictures of Mata Hari.

"I'm reading about spies; this one had the code name H-21."

"It's easy to see how she got her information," our father said; then, he took off his coat and stared into the fire the way we all stare into the ocean when we're at home.

In the evening, we were in the lounge listening to a folk singer play a dulcimer when Beth began to complain about her ankle.

"It throbs," she said, "like it has its own heart."

"We should take her to the clinic," our mother said to me, and we left our father sitting alone in the tap room with red carpeting, his beer on the table in a sweaty bottle.

Because ski accidents were frequent, the lodge had its own doctor. Before we could see him, my mother and Beth and I spent time in a waiting room with outdated magazines and photographs of mountain ranges; our mother filled out a series of forms and was called several times to a window where a woman was filing her fingernails. Beth and I found ourselves marooned beside a lady with a fussy toddler, across from a man who seemed to cough in paragraphs.

"Frances?" the nurse called, and our mother stood up but Beth continued to sit.

"She likes to be called Beth," our mother told the nurse, "She doesn't use the first name on the insurance card."

"What seems to be troubling Frances?" the nurse asked when we got into the exam room.

"She hurt her ankle skiing," our mother said.

Beth looked at the floor. "I ran into a tree."

After taking Beth's height and weight, the nurse disappeared down a corridor, and the three of us were left alone.

The doctor arrived, holding a clipboard. "How is Frances feeling?" he said.

That night, after Beth had been x-rayed and wrapped in a bandage and told to stay off her ankle, we returned to our cabin where our father was tending the fire with a poker.

"The Inuit have fifty words for snow," our father said.

"How do you know?" Beth said

"The man who plays the dulcimer; he was full of facts. I can also tell you how a dulcimer is made."

"I can live without knowing that," our mother said, flinging off her shoes.